I0618645

Copyright © 2020 Simone Luxe

ISBN: 978-1-67802-648-6

Publisher: Simone Luxe Books

https://simoneluxebooks.wixsite.com/thedolls

DON'T BREAK THE DOLLS

Scarlet's Story

by Simone Luxe

ADULT CONTENT

This book depicts acts of violence and sexual situations. It might be a trigger for some and is **not** appropriate for everyone.

Children should **not** read it.

People who are easily offended by people, places and events that include (but are not limited to): swearing, strippers, prostitutes, empowered women, empowered men dressed as empowered women, lesbians, bisexuals, drug use, sex, nudity and/or murder should **not** read it.... because in this book, these things are often happening simultaneously.

This book depicts fictional people, places and events. Any similarity between actual people, places and/or events is an unfortunate coincidence. Please do NOT try to recreate ANY of the events or acts in this book.

You are responsible for your own actions.

While the people, places and events in this book are fictional, domestic violence is real. Human trafficking is real. If you or someone you know is experiencing violence or trafficking, please contact a shelter, outreach program, the local police and/or one of the toll-free hotline numbers listed at the end of this book.

This book is dedicated to the beaten, the broken and the damned. We may not be in this together…but none of us are in it alone.

-Simone Luxe

BOOK ONE

"Look at me.

Do you see me? I was beautiful once. Shiny hair and a magic in my eyes that drew everyone in. Can you still see it? No, I know you can't. That was another time. Now I am only made up of shadows and memories that linger in the minds of men.

Sit with me.

I have a story to tell. It has The Trifecta (needed for a great story): love, laughs and death. Every genre has this Trifecta. Art imitates life and every life has The Three. It is rarely a balance. You'll get more of one than the others. My wish for you is that your story doesn't hang as heavily upon death as mine.

My story begins and ends with death. Fair warning: the death that comes at the end is mine. Don't be upset. After all, that is how all our stories end. For me, it will always be a welcomed ending to a damned existence; a death befitting the life I lived.

Stay with me.

It will be worth it. You'll see. It is human nature to long for the stories of others' lives. We want to see every skeleton in every closet...except our own, of course. No one wants to pull the tangled bones from their own closet. I spent every living day hoping that mine wouldn't come dancing out at the wrong time, telling the world my secrets.

Close your eyes.

Deep breath. In and out. The sweet smell in the lightest of breezes…that's honeysuckle. There was nothing quite like the aroma of honeysuckle when the wind blew. It wasn't just that it outranked the usual smell of stale cigarette smoke and alcohol that I was accustomed to. There was more to it than that. It reminded me of a woman I never really knew.

Open your eyes.

We're here. Small Impoverished Deep Southern Town, USA. Ever been here? From the looks of your Armani suit, I'd say, probably not.

The air is wet here. It is heavy and thick with humidity and if you aren't careful you can drown simply trying to breathe. Look 'round….lots of people are drowning 'round here….and, yes, there's the accent. It always sneaks back in at the worst of times. That slow drawl that makes me sound like I grew up in the woods.

Do you see me?

That's me, over there (or should I say 'then'?), in the field. So beautiful. So sad and afraid of everything. This isn't the very beginning…it is just the beginning of the story I'm telling today. How old do I look to you there? You can't tell? Men had a hard time telling my age back then or maybe they didn't care. Even now, I'm not sure which it was. I didn't have anyone, you see. No one to tell me that they would come for me….that I would be fighting men off me my entire life.

My mother died when I was two years old. I don't remember much about her except the few buried moments that pop up in my memory now and then. I remember how she would sing to me while we picked honeysuckle from the bushes. While I was still at my father's, in my dreams, she often showed up to save me from the monsters my mind manifested while I slept.

…but she was a manifestation too. In my waking life, she never came to save me, of course. No one did. I was beaten by my father, violated by many men…tortured in my life and in my soul for the 13 long years after my mother died. There, in that field, I am fifteen years old…and I am only minutes away from a descent into madness that I never recovered from.

Watch my (her) face.

It will change momentarily, from sad and damaged to determined and bold. Something inside me (her) breaks…but then is masterfully rebuilt in only….there it is!

Did you see it? Something in that mind flipped on like a switch. I am overjoyed even now watching it happen from this perspective, from the outside. A different, stronger person will now rise out of that field and walk toward her destiny. Come on! We have to follow her!"

"Where are we going?"

"Ah, so you do speak. I was beginning to wonder if you still had a voice or if we were both going to tire of hearing only mine. We are going to witness the death that begins my story. We are going to watch her father die."

Chapter 1: Come Sunday Morning

She stood up in the field and walked toward the broken-down shack with the grace she was known to have. Her movements were fluid, almost like she was dancing in water with every move she made.

She pulled her long, black hair into a ponytail, then wound it tightly with her fingers into a bun at the back of her head. If there was one thing her father taught her, it was that your hair couldn't be down if there was a possibility of a fight. Someone may grab it and render you useless with a single tug.

He had done this very thing to her many times before she learned that valuable lesson.

With her hair pulled back, her pale skin was visible and showed the signs of abuse. There was a bruise on the side of her face and scrapes around her neck.

Her dress was white and shapeless with spaghetti straps. Her bare arms, no longer covered by her flowing locks, were visibly showing varying degrees of hurt and healing in spots of purple and green.

Her crystal eyes were glazed with leftover tears, but no new tears were forming. Something within her was building a wall around her for protection. Onlookers couldn't see it, but it was there.

"Bless her heart," a lady said as she and her friend sat in their rocking chairs and watched the damaged girl emerge from the field.

"Someone oughta do somethin', don't ya think? Poor thang."

….but no one spoke up.

No one stepped forward.

Everyone in the town knew the story of the old man and the girl at 1515 Briarberry. In a small place like that, everyone knows everything about everybody. As was the way in small towns in that time and place, long before cell phones and internet closed the gaps in communication and knowledge, gossip happened in hushed tones on porch swings and after church on Sundays.

….and no one wanted to get involved in another family's business.

So, on that Saturday in the heat of June, they only watched and listened to the usual noises of violent chaos coming from the home that looked like it should have caved in on itself years ago. They watched and listened, taking mental notes to tell their friends.

Tomorrow was Sunday, after all.

It would turn out to be quite an exciting Sunday, indeed. Everyone would have conflicting ideas and observations would be recounted again and again in the years to come, but what was certain: come Sunday morning, the old man was dead, and the girl was gone.

. . . .

Two boys walked down a dirt road with large trees on either side.

Their shoes were covered in mud from playing at the creek and felt as though they were getting heavier with every step. Their skin, wet and wrinkled like raisins, had only just begun to dry in the sun. One of the boys had his shirt thrown over his shoulder and the other had his draped around his neck.

It was the first time either of their parents let them out by themselves since their middle-of-nowhere town had been rocked to its core by the murder of a man and the disappearance of his daughter.

It had been two months and other than a bloodstained dress that washed up on the riverbank, there were no leads.

"My uncle said he saw her leaving the house and she was drenched in blood. He said he knows she's the one that done it."

"Can't be. My daddy said he was first on tha' scene and looked like two or three men got a holt of tha' old man. No way that girl coulda done it. She weighed 110 soaking wet if she weighed a pound."

"Your daddy was there? Is it true what they said about the walls? Did someone...."

"Play in the old man's blood? Yep. I'm tellin' ya', no way it was that girl. She was scared of her own shadow and 'specially scared of that old man. I think whoever did it took her with 'em."

"If they did take her, couldn't be any worse than what was already happening to her in that house."

"Yeah..."

Simultaneously, they picked up their pace and neither boy spoke the rest of the way home.

• • • • • • •

She vaguely remembers the blood. There had been a lot of it. She washed it off her body in the river, removed her dress and watched it float away.

She had a small bag with a few clothes and some money she had been taking – little by little - from her father's pocket when he was passed out from the whiskey.

She dressed herself in fresh clothing and walked down the river until the sun disappeared and she found herself enveloped in darkness. After changing course, she found a road and eventually a man in a light blue pickup truck offered her a ride.

He looked older than her, of course, but still young, likely in his twenties. He was dressed in worn work jeans and a faded red shirt with the sleeves cut off. He tipped his straw cowboy hat to her.

"Where you headed, darlin'?"

She thought about that for a moment. Her head felt like it was stuffed with cotton and her memory felt blurry. She felt as though she were trapped in a dream.

She knew with certainty her father was dead. She had been there when it happened, and she had escaped. She felt a great sense of relief in that.

For the first time in her life, she was free.

…but where would she go?

"Wherever you're headed," she finally answered in a voice that barely sounded like her own.

He smiled, tipped his hat again and said, "hop on in, then. We're going to N'Awlins!"

…….

He was on the run from his future, in the summer of 1974, when he picked up a girl to keep him company on his drive to New Orleans, Louisiana. His father wanted him to take over the family business in Tennessee, but he had bigger dreams for himself than to live and die in the town he was born in.

It was the middle of the night when he saw her in the distance. There was no civilization around for miles, so he wasn't sure exactly where she came from.

When he asked all she said was, "it doesn't matter 'cause I'm never goin' back".

It was dark inside the truck, but he could tell she was pretty. He tried to coax her to move closer, but she stayed where she was and looked out the window. When they stopped for gas and some snacks, he saw her in the light for the first time.

She was mesmerizing.

She noticed him staring and locked eyes with his. Her eyes were probing for an answer to a question she hadn't asked yet.

"How old do you think I am?"

"I dunno. Early to mid- twenties, like me," he answered still stuck in her powerful gaze. "I'll be 25 next month."

"I'm fifteen," she shot back almost daring him to follow up with an inappropriate comment.

There was fire in her eyes now.

"Good Lawd....I'm sorry...," he stumbled over his words and shifted uncomfortably from one foot to the other.

She relaxed her shoulders.

"I apologize sincerely if I made you uncomfortable. It's just...I had no idea. My Gawd, what are you doing coming out of the woods in the middle of nowhere...and why would you get into a truck with a stranger? What if I was a murderer or somethin'? Dammit, girl! Your parents know where you are?"

"Name's Scarlet and I don't have any parents. I don't have a home or anywhere to go."

She spoke sincerely as the fire subsided from her eyes and then she did something that surprised both of them.

She laughed.

. . . .

Over a 12-hour period, Scarlet witnessed a death and escaped her own, found freedom from her lunatic father and stumbled across the first decent man she had ever met.

"I go by Leo," he had told her as they drove, "short for Leonard. Who the hell names a baby Leonard?"

Scarlet laughed again. Laughing felt good. Had she ever really laughed before?

Leo took a joint from his cigarette pack and sparked the end with an old Zippo. He inhaled deeply and let it out slowly, filling the cab with smoke. Scarlet watched the cloud dance in and out of itself, then put her hand out but he shook his head.

"I'm not smoking a doobie with you, kiddo. You'll run across plenty of it in your life, but you won't get it from me. If you smoke, it needs to be with people your own age and you should wait until you are old enough to handle it."

He expected her to protest, but she only smiled and watched the smoke dissipate.

They rode in silence for a little while before he asked, "so what are you going to do when you get to N'Awlins, Scarlet? I don't feel right 'bout leavin' you but I wouldn't feel right 'bout takin' you 'round the people and places I know either."

"I'll be just fine, Leo," she answered with confidence. "What I'm runnin' to can't be any worse than what I'm runnin' from."

"What are you runnin' from?"

After a moment of looking out the window as if she expected the answer to be written somewhere in the stars, she looked at Leo and said, "myself."

"Well, darlin', you can't run from yourself. You'll be runnin' your whole life."

"Yes," she answered. "Probably."

......

Scarlet pulled her hair into a ponytail. Her window was rolled down, and she was leaning on the edge of the door, with a smile on her face. She watched the world rush by her. She had never felt this kind of freedom.

At the next stop, Leo pumped gas and paused at Scarlet's window when he saw her entire face in the light for the first time.

She had a bruise on the left side and scratches on her neck.

She was wearing jeans and a long sleeve shirt – even though it was the middle of summer in the south. Leo began to piece it all together.

"You wanna talk about that?" he asked, motioning to her face.

"Nope," Scarlet answered looking through his eyes and into his soul.

Leo internally struggled with his place in this young woman's life for a moment…but then he decided to let it go. If she was running from the person who gave her those injuries, then it was probably best that he was helping her flee.

"You want a burger?" he asked as if the previous conversation hadn't even happened.

"I don't eat meat," Scarlet said, smiling, "but I'll take some fries and a strawberry shake."

"You got it, kid," Leo said before he winked and walked away.

Scarlet leaned back in the seat and put her feet up on the dash. She felt…happy. She felt safe. She couldn't recall ever feeling this way. She finally had a chance to have a real life outside the walls that had imprisoned her.

She was finally free of the **man** who had imprisoned her.

…and he could never find her to take her back.

He was dead.

Thank God, she thought. *Thank you, God. He is dead.*

She had never believed in God…at least not in the one other people seemed to believe in.

…but there, in that moment, Scarlet believed.

Chapter 2: Friday Night Fantasies

The first few years in New Orleans were a blur of new people, places and experiences. Maybe the drugs were a factor or maybe because everything happened so quickly it was hard to keep track of specific memories.

New Orleans was the perfect place for a runaway in those days. The underbelly of a society all its own welcomed her in, taught her to provide for herself and became her home.

Building on the political and social changes of the sixties, the seventies were a time of continued progression in America. The sexual revolution was in full swing. The fight for civil rights was still underway and second-wave feminism was spreading into suburbia.

Movies, television and music took the flashiness of the decade's trends to a new level and bodies – young and old - moved sensually all night, under neon lights and disco balls.

Alcohol, drugs and cigarettes were in the hands and mouths of an entire generation that had chosen to live only in the moment. Disco Biscuits were washed down with Pink Squirrels, everyone had Grass in their pockets and White Lady was the intoxicant of the elite.

When people asked her where she was from, Scarlet would always say, "I'm from the streets. That's where I learned who I wanted to be and who I didn't want to be. That's where I grew up."

…but she wasn't just from any streets.

She was from the streets of New Orleans.

For Scarlet and her friends, there was no better place to be. Carnival, Bourbon Street, Jazz Fest in Congo Square, Pontchartrain Beach, Drag at Les Pierres...their city was their eternal playground.

They were young, beautiful and they had the world at their feet.

......

Five years after Leo reluctantly dropped her off at a busy street corner, she stood on the balcony of her apartment and felt so restless she thought she might spin right off the edge of the Earth.

"What's got you down, doll?"

Scarlet turned toward the question and ran face first into Valentina's chest.

"Damn, honey, if you want to eat my tits, just ask," Valentina said. She flashed her brilliant smile and adjusted herself. "Otherwise you'll just knock them around and they will end up on my shoulders."

Valentina's gown was silver and shiny like a disco ball. It dipped in the front and didn't have a back. She had just put on the matching shoes.

Scarlet's best friend always said his transformation was never complete until he put his heels on. Once the heels were on, the already tall Val became the gorgeous, show-stopping Valentina and until Scarlet put her own heels on, Valentina's boobs would be all she would see.

"No one ever taught me how to be a lady, so I had no choice but to be a woman instead," Scarlet said helping Valentina adjust her cleavage.

"Oh, baby, you know I feel the same way. You need a drink and toke….and a shower, girl. What have you been doing all day? You know the moon is shining, so that means so are we," Valentina flipped her long blonde hair over her smooth toffee-colored shoulder.

"Now, let's go get some men…."

"…to give us their money," finished Scarlet with a smile and a wink.

"Yes, bitch. Money. All the money. Now, get your sexy ass moving. It is Friday night in N'Awlins, baby!"

....

The lights were low, but his voice was loud, "…knew from the second I saw you…not just because you are the sexiest thing I've ever seen…"

Scarlet pretended to listen, but these conversations were starting to feel like they were stuck on some kind of loop. Every night, the same conversation with different faces. She looked around at all the men in the strip club. These men were from different backgrounds and they came from different places.

Could none of them come up with something original to say?

She continued to smoke her cigarette, rolling the smooth stick between her fingers and pressing it to her glossy lips.

Inhale.

Exhale.

Slow and methodical, the way she did everything, she watched the smoke linger in the air.

Inhale.

Exhale.

His hair was too perfect. There was not one hair out of place. It looked like a fucking helmet.

Pay attention, Scarlet, she thought. *Stop looking at his hair helmet. Every bill in his wallet is for you if you can just focus, girl.*

"...I could tell from our first conversation that you were so smart. I knew you were Ivy League..."

She batted her lashes and pursed her lips for another inhale. She had a part to play. She had to be the illusion. The fantasy is what they came for.

"...you just aren't like the others. The rest of these girls...I mean, you just don't belong here..."

I wonder if his wife picked out those clothes or if it was his mother. Either way there is a woman behind it. There always is. I bet they didn't advise him to leave the first four buttons unbuttoned. No one should have that much chest hair on display.

"…and those eyes…"

That one was true. She was well-known for her eyes. She had a penetrating gaze that made men feel like they were the only person in the room. Some said they felt like she could look all the way inside their soul. Her green eyes made men fall in love…but more importantly (to her), her sexy stare made them reach deep into their pockets for her.

The downside to having "eyes made of magic" (…*ugh is that really what he just said?*) was that it confused them into an intimacy that didn't exist and sometimes lead them to reveal secrets about themselves that she didn't want to know.

"…one time in the back with one of these whores…"

Scarlet came back from her daze and snapped, "what did you say?"

He stared with confusion.

"I asked you a question. What the fuck did you just say?"

He replied, "I was telling you about this girl that I met here…."

"No, you didn't say 'girl'. What did you call her?"

He started to repeat himself but didn't have the opportunity to finish because Scarlet put her cigarette out on his hairy ass chest.

. . . .

"His watch costed more than my car, Scarlet!"

"Cost."

"What?"

"Cost, sugar. His watch **cost** more than your car. 'Costed' isn't a word," Scarlet replied calmly as she applied more gloss to her lips.

She was leaning over the counter looking into the mirror, occasionally glancing up and into the eyes of her co-worker who was doing the same beside her.

"Yeah, well, we can't all be as smart as you, now can we? ...or apparently as rich. I can't believe you did that. The manager's gonna be pissed...and yeah, I said 'gonna', Scarlet!"

Scarlet smiled in the mirror at Mica. Poor pretty baby. She reminded Scarlet a little of her younger self, when she first started in the clubs, but Mica had worse grammar and a way better ass. Scarlet had worked hard to ditch the southern drawl she had when she first arrived in New Orleans. The accent she had now couldn't really be traced to a particular area of the county nor dialect of any group.

The busty blonde, Mica, was still excited to be here making more money than she had ever seen in her young life. She didn't yet understand that the clubs needed her more than she needed the clubs. She didn't realize that she was the show so she could make the rules.

Scarlet returned her attention to her own appearance and ran her fingers through the loose curls that fell to her waist. Her hair was dark and her skin creamy white. Even without the black liner and mascara, her eyes, bright green with yellow circling the pupil, caught everyone's attention.

She liked her pouty lips to be painted with a certain shade of red. She turned to the side, smoothing her dress over her hips and admiring her curves. She had come to love the hourglass body that had felt like a curse in her youth.

"What if you get fired?" Mica asked with true concern.

Scarlet looked around the dressing room. It was long and narrow; painted an awful shade of green over the top of an even worse shade of yellow. Mirrors hung along the right side of the wall with lights bolted across the top. The lockers were lined up on the left. It smelled of hairspray and cheap perfume.

I fucking wish I could get out of this shithole that easily, Scarlet thought.

She took one last glance in the mirror, turned to face Mica and said, "they won't fire me, dollface. Now, get your hot ass back to work. You can't make any money in the dressing room."

....

Sam's office looked like a strip club office: wood paneling and cheap art in cheap frames on every wall. It was dim, dank and dreary.

Scarlet sat in a chair opposite Sam's desk, watching the cigar smoke billowing around her boss's head. She knew his mouth was moving somewhere underneath all the smoke.

He was rattling on when she noticed for the first time that he looked a lot like the portrait of a pale-faced Jesus that hung in the entry of a church she had attended once, when she was still on the streets.

She laughed out loud.

"This is no laughing matter, Scarlet!"

She hadn't been paying much attention to what he had been saying, but she realized that Strip Club Jesus was wearing a very serious facial expression, so she attempted to poise herself and find a serious face of her own.

"You can't fucking burn people…what the…."

The smoke was clearing, and Jesus began to look much more like Sam, the owner of the club and Scarlet's biggest fan. She did make him a lot of money, after all.

She had been in and out of this office for similar conversations many times over the years, so it seemed odd she had never noticed how much Sam favored Jesus…or how much Jesus favored Sam.

"…the last time, Scarlet. I mean it! Jesus Christ!"

Scarlet tried to stay composed but couldn't help herself and she giggled again.

"Get out of my fucking office, Scarlet! You are fucking killing me!"

Scarlet smiled and walked over to Sam. She pulled a small silver vile from her wristlet and offered him a bump. Then she did one herself.

"Calm down, honey. He was an asshole. He called one of the girls a whore."

"Well, which one? …because dammit, Scarlet, some of them are!"

She did another bump and held one under his nostril. He pressed his finger to the opposite side of his nose and snorted loudly.

"I know, Sam-baby," she said, stroking his hair, "but only **we** get to say it."

. . . .

Scarlet and Val sat on her bed, sorting their money.

"You **burned** him?" Val asked giggling. "Girl, I know Sam has had enough of your ass."

"Girl...you know Sam **loves** this ass," Scarlet said turning hers toward Val.

He slapped it and they both laughed.

Val and Scarlet had been inseparable for years. They met when they were both on the streets and they helped lift each other up and into an extravagant apartment with an extravagant life.

Their two-bedroom corner apartment was in a sought-after area with a perfect view of all the best parades during Carnival. They had luxe velvet furniture, a papasan chair and the walls were covered with colorful art pieces from local artists. The floor had a fluffy shag rug and they turned their sunroom into an indoor garden with macramé planters.

Their wrought iron balcony wrapped around the corner so both Scarlet and Val had a door leading out from their bedrooms. At night, they could leave their windows open and let the jazz music from a nearby club lull them to sleep.

After work, they always ended up in Scarlet's room, spreading their bills out on the bed and sharing stories of their escapades.

Sometimes, even though they had all that space and their own rooms, Val would still sleep in Scarlet's bed with her. They were both dazzling and confident on the outside but underneath, they were still two broken street kids just trying to get through the night.

…sharing their day's earnings and one sleeping bag.

Chapter 3: The Puppeteer

Scarlet walked through every room like she owned it.

She commanded attention with every step, every movement of her perfectly manicured hands and every word she spoke. She was a carefully created masterpiece. She knew exactly what to say and how to say it. There was nothing she wanted that she didn't have or couldn't get…and that included people.

She preferred sex with women but enjoyed having a man tied to her bedpost occasionally. She had never had a romantic relationship with either a man or a woman and she didn't want one. There was nothing appealing to her about being with the same person for too many nights in a row, let alone a year or a lifetime.

(Sometimes life has a different plan for us.)

So, when Scarlet's eyes met Vasco's across a room at a New Year's Eve party on December 31, 1979 and time stopped, she didn't have a full concept of what was happening. He was the most stunning man she had ever seen. Her stomach flipped over, and she started sweating.

"I think the coke is bad," she said in a panicked voice to Val, grabbing his hand.

"Uh-uh…it's de-light-ful!" Val exclaimed, throwing his hands in the air and tilting his head back. He spun in a circle and squealed.

When he finished his one-person celebration, he looked at Scarlet and followed her gaze, still speaking, "what's wrong with you…who are you looking at….oooooh, girl! Yaaaaahs! He's prrrretty…and straight. I can tell by the way he's looking at you like he's going to eat you. Go on over there and get eaten, baby!"

Val smacked her on the ass and Scarlet, startled, almost lost her balance.

"If you don't go get him, I'm going to go get him and bring him over here," Val said as he waved at him and yelled, "'he-ey, handsome!" across the room.

Scarlet tried to leave but Val had a death grip on her hand and wouldn't let her go.

"I think I'm going to throw up. I think it's the coke," Scarlet whispered.

"Don't be silly. We don't do bad coke. You're just smitten, kitten," he said to her.

He smiled. Val had the most beautiful, perfect teeth and his smile was contagious…but this time, Scarlet wasn't smiling.

She was dying…she was sure of it.

Val was calling again, "come here, baby!...no, not you, ew, why would I call you?" he asked, disgusted, shooing away a man who had started toward them. "You there, with the eyes….yaaahs, you! Someone over here wants to meet you, honey!"

Scarlet's face felt hot and her palms were sweating.

I don't sweat, she thought. *I'm going to die. It's a heart attack or something. Oh, no…here he comes. Oh my god…Val! If I don't die, I'm going to punch Val in the dick!*

"Hello, gorgeous! Meet Scarlet. Scarlet meet Gorgeous! I need a drink. See you later, lovers," Val was already sashaying away before he finished his sentence.

Those eyes…Scarlet could not stop looking at his eyes. Everything around them seemed to slow down. She never wanted to stop looking at his face. As the countdown to ring in a new decade began, the party was going wild, but for Scarlet and Vasco, they were the only two people in the entire world.

. . . .

Scarlet and Vasco developed a love that was passionate and deep.

Vasco was tall with dark curly hair, amber skin and hazelnut eyes. His playful dimples made Scarlet melt and when he wrapped his arms around her, his muscular build made her feel protected from the world.

He was her everything and she was his.

So, later that year, when Val packed up Valentina to take her to a show in Los Angeles, it was only natural that Vasco moved into Scarlet's apartment the same day.

In a time and place where drug use was the norm, their lives were full of late nights getting high with friends and parties with strangers. Their apartment became a hotspot for impresarios, DJs, musicians and poets.

They would watch parades from their balcony and throw beads during Mardi Gras. The music…oh, the music they could hear coming from their city as they danced into the morning.

They traveled to California the following year to see Valentina. Her show was divine, and the young couple couldn't be happier for her.

Los Angeles had an entirely new scene for them to explore and so many beautiful people to meet. They went to several local clubs and after losing Val somewhere amongst his new circle of friends, Scarlet and Vasco had sex on the balcony of their hotel.

It was a night to remember.

When they returned to their home in New Orleans, they tried to settle back into their lives, but their visit to California had started a longing for travel and for new experiences. They bought a map of the U.S. and spent the week marking the places they wanted to go together.

"I want to go everywhere," Scarlet said excitedly. "I want to go everywhere and see everything!"

Vasco admired her child-like excitement about life. She portrayed herself to the world as cool and enigmatic, but behind closed doors she was adventurous, playful and funny. Sometimes, when they were listening to a song she liked, she would grab any nearby object that even remotely resembled a microphone and serenade him with an over-the-top performance that either left them laughing or lead them straight to the bedroom.

Even when she stood in front of him, wearing only panties and a t shirt, no makeup, hair a mess from a crazy night of drugs, drinking and sex, he was positive that she was the most beautiful woman in the world. They were a young couple in love and excited about the lifetime of adventure ahead of them.

…but sometimes life has a different plan for us.

....

Over the course of her life, Scarlet would wonder many times if it would have been different had she been there.

Could she have stopped it from happening?

Was it, like the beginning of her life, some sort of destiny mapped out by the stars that she couldn't control? If so, who was pulling the fucking strings on this shitshow? Could she one day, find The Puppeteer and make him endure the pain of suffering he had brought upon her with his sick storyline?

She did get to tell the love of her life goodbye, at least. The sadist in charge of her experiences allowed her to look into his eyes one last time. As his energy left his body and disappeared into nowhere, she clutched his hand and cried out with an animalistic scream that is only heard in moments of extreme torture.

The nurses were kind enough to let her lay with Vasco's bloody, bandaged body after he died. Scarlet cried until her tears ran dry and then she became very still, longing to just die with him.

Her lover, her best friend, her partner in crime, her everything…was gone and she didn't have the will to go on without him.

She somehow made it through the funeral but declined invitations from friends to stay with them and returned to her apartment to grieve in her own way.

She put on Vasco's clothes and laid on the floor in the middle of the room. She couldn't remember how long she was there. Night turned into day and then back into night, but she couldn't remember how many times.

The heavy blanket of depression wrapped itself around her shoulders, forcing her body downward into despair and sending her mind into darkness. She had never known this kind of loneliness...not even in the isolated captivity that had been her childhood.

When the phone rang, she was startled out of her shadowy downward spiral. She wanted to continue to stay right where she was, but she already knew who was calling. She made it to the phone, pulled it from the table and into the floor. She held the receiver to her ear and heard the familiar voice...the only voice left that sounded like home.

"You ok, sugar?"

"No," Scarlet replied in a voice that was harsh and dry.

"I'm so sorry, baby girl," Val's voice soothed over the line.

"Come get me. I can't leave. This is the only place I can still feel him...even if it's just a little bit now."

"Oh, honey, I would already be there....but....well, I didn't want to tell you like this....but, I'm sick, girl. They don't know what it is yet. I've been in and out of the hospital. The doctor wants me to go in today….and…I don't think I'll make it back out again this time, Scarlet."

Scarlet bolted upright and tears that she didn't know she had left streamed down her face.

The director of her life was indeed a twisted son-of-a-bitch.

……..

On the plane ride to California, Scarlet replayed every moment she had ever had with Val.

From their first meeting on a street corner when they were 15 all the way up until the day they moved into their apartment. The parties, the laughing, the crying…every moment spent together…

Vasco had been the love of her life and her best friend…but Val was more than just a best friend. He had been her brother and her sister. He had been her mom, dad, cousin, uncle and auntie. Her only real family for years, he had played every role in her life she had needed.

Val was her life companion and she was his.

When she lost her way and life was too dark, Val was the sun, the moon and the stars that showed her the way back to the path again.

"Time to shine," he would say, throwing open her curtains if she'd been 'under the blankets' for too many days.

'Under the blankets' was their chosen phrase to use instead of depression. They thought it sounded more socially acceptable and definitely sexier.

"You've been in there long enough," he would say. "Time to bless the world with your fine ass again…plus I need you to do my lashes, bitch."

He would pull the blankets off.

…play bongos on her ass cheeks.

… lay beside her and sing in her face.

She would protest…but in the end, she always got up for him.

Even now, she was only up because of him.

…but what would she do when he was gone?

Chapter 4: Final Curtain

Scarlet arrived at the hospital to a scene worse than any she had expected. The nurses were covered from head to toe in hazmat gear and they advised her not to go into the room with Val.

"I just lost the love of my life and will soon lose my dearest friend. I am much more afraid of living than I am of dying. So, please, get the fuck out of my way," Scarlet spoke with a smile, but her eyes were wild.

They stepped aside, trying to hand her a suit for protection but she smacked it away and entered the room.

Once inside, Scarlet leaned against the closed door with relief and muttered, "what a fucking cunt…"

"Me or the nurse, honey?" Val's voice sounded shaky and distant.

"Oh, Val…" Scarlet started with a half-smile.

The room was dim, but she could see his outline in the hospital bed. Tubes ran in and out of his body and something was making a low, beeping noise in the background.

She walked toward him and could see the lesions on his body…that is, what was left of his body. He was a mere skeleton with skin stretched across his bones. He looked so small and fragile laying there by himself.

"My beautiful Val," she let the tears fall as she reached out to rest her hand on his face.

"You are the only beauty left, doll," he weakly motioned to his appearance.

"No," she slowly shook her head and wiped her face. She picked up the suitcase she had practically thrown on the floor when she arrived and continued, "I brought my bag of tricks. You aren't going out like this."

The smile was a fraction of Val's gleaming smile she had known and loved for so many years, but it was a smile just the same.

Death was coming, they could both feel it, but they still had a few moments left until the curtain dropped on their time together.

. . . .

Sometimes, while her friend was resting, Scarlet would check in on some of the other patients that didn't have any visitors. Prior to her arrival, the nurses had watched so many men die alone with even their own mothers and fathers refusing to see them.

Scarlet wasn't just an exception to the norm; she was a light in the darkness. She was an angel to those men on the cursed floor of the hospital.

The nurses peeked in occasionally to watch Scarlet and Val. Some with judgement, but most in awe at the young woman who seemed to be the only person who wasn't afraid of the disease that was gripping the gay men of Los Angeles. They finally knew that it wasn't "gay cancer" as they had originally thought, but there was still confusion as to how and why it spread.

Scarlet didn't care about any of that as she cleaned her friend carefully and dressed him in a pink satin robe with matching turban. She propped him up with pillows and helped him position himself so there was room for her to sit opposite him. Then she covered his face in makeup and showed him in the mirror. He held the handle with a shaking hand and looked both excited and disappointed. He said something inaudible and they both laughed.

The older nurse watching them through the glass pressed her hand to her heart. She had many opportunities over the years to witness displays of affection, but these two really tugged at her emotions. She was so enthralled with her peeping that she was startled when she heard a voice behind her.

"I think I smell marijuana. Are they smoking marijuana in there, Susan?"

"Oh, stop it, Sara!" the aging lady answered, a little embarrassed that she was caught spying. "Let them have their fun while they can. He doesn't have much longer."

The younger nurse thought it over for a moment and finally asked rhetorically, "it is sad, isn't it?"

The two nurses stood side by side looking in at Scarlet and Val for a little while longer, then without a word they went their separate ways to check on the other patients in the hall.

. . . .

"Cut your eyes to the side and check again, princess. They still there?"

"No," Scarlet answered with a smile.

"It's about time. I thought they were just going to keep standing there all damn day like they never seen a beautiful man in makeup before. Let's have another toke, girl."

Scarlet put the pipe up to her friend's lips, then her own and they both watched the smoke roll around the room.

"I'm going to miss this," Val said, smiling at his friend.

Scarlet's eyes began to feel wet and she said, "please don't, I can't...."

"No, honey. There is no crying-. We aren't going to fuck up this mascara. It is what it is, though, baby. The applause and cheers are over and there is no encore...but that's not what I'm going to miss."

"Don't you dare fucking say it...." The words caught in Scarlet's throat as she tried to fight the tears spilling over her lashes.

"I'm going to miss you, you sexy bitch...more than the stage, the sun and all the stars over N'Awlins."

They held hands, looked into each other's eyes and, despite Val's previous statement, they both fucked up their mascara.

....

Scarlet spent every day at the hospital and toward the very end, many evenings, as well. It always hurt her to walk down the hall and see another patient's door open, the bed empty.

One by one, the men were taken by the death they knew they could not escape.

Scarlet and the nurses mourned for them with a silent nod during eye contact as they passed one another. They all knew it was only a matter of time, but that didn't make it any less painful when the time came.

Scarlet was there when the imminent end of life came for her dear Val. She closed her eyes and longed for death to take her too, just as she had with Vasco. She thought of Val, Vasco and the mother she couldn't remember.

Please, she thought, *don't leave me here alone again.*

...but when she opened her eyes, she was alone. A body remained, but Val —and Valentina- were gone.

Chapter 5: Walker's Blonde

Scarlet made one trip back to New Orleans with Val's ashes, per his last wishes but she couldn't bear to stay longer than a few days. It didn't feel like home anymore.

She said goodbye to the people and places that she'd known…to the memories that lingered on every corner. Then, just as she had with her birthplace and childhood home, she pushed the city to the back of her mind and started over.

She cut and dyed her hair into a style that fit the times. She drank every night she worked and tried a variety of drugs that made their way through the clubs.

There were several good things about being a dancer in the strip clubs during those days. Scarlet's favorite: you could walk out in the middle of the night, never to be seen again and no one thought anything of it. They just assumed you moved on to the next club or town…and that is exactly what she did.

A new town, a new name and a new look whenever the notion struck her.

She visited a lot of the cities that she and Vasco had marked on the map. The map was one of the few things she had taken with her from New Orleans when she left. There was a bittersweet feeling as she left each city behind and a feeling of hope that the next might feel like home.

…but nowhere ever felt like home.

New Orleans had been...but most of what made it that way was Vasco and Val. They had been her family...and now she didn't have one.

So, unfulfilled, she moved onto the next place.

She was leaving a strip club in Tennessee where she had been playing the part of Roni, a blonde, when she happened upon someone near a dumpster. The young woman was on the ground crying, her skirt was lifted, and she wasn't wearing any panties.

"You ok over there, honey..." Scarlet trailed off as she edged closer.

She could see it was one of the girls from the club and it was clear she had been raped. Scarlet bent down, looked into her frightened blue eyes and calmly continued, "who was it? Where did he go?"

The young woman stuttered from shock when she tried to speak but she was able to give Scarlet a name and point in the direction he had gone after the attack.

Scarlet helped her to her feet, and they walked back toward the club. Once inside, Scarlet pushed the woman's hair back from her face and told her everything was going to be ok.

"Are you guys going to do something about this?" Scarlet hissed at the bouncer once they were out of earshot.

He stood with his arms crossed. The only thing tighter than his jeans was his white t-shirt. His sandy blonde hair was messy, and though his eyes were full of concern, his words were not.

"We tell the girls not to see anyone outside of here, Roni. This is why."

"I don't give a fuck about your rules. You know who he is. She knows his name. She said he comes in here all the time," Scarlet's eyes were searing through him.

"Yeah, but…Roni, wait…."

It was too late for excuses. Roni had already turned on her heel and was slamming the door.

•••••••

In the days before cameras stood watch to recount the moves of patrons, it was easy to slip into and out of a bar without many people being able to recollect exactly what happened. When the police asked questions later, "hot blonde" was the only thing anyone could recall about the evening.

"Her eyes were amazin'," the bartender offered.

"Incredible ass," one of the regular barflies chimed in.

"Nice big tits too," said another.

"So, we are looking for…a hot blonde…with big tits …and a great ass?" the detective asked irritably.

"…with amazin' eyes," the bartender added as if that somehow changed everything.

The detective left the dive bar more confused than when he arrived. He got into the car with his partner and vented about "drunken idiots" and "dead ends" and finished up with "hot blonde, my ass!"

"Didn't go well?" his partner, the younger of the two men, asked.

"No. Last person he was seen with was a hot blonde with a great ass…oh, and don't forget 'amazin' eyes'! Everyone in there was three sheets to the wind that night. Ain't no hot blonde going to be hanging out with a sonofabitch like Eugene Walker in a shithole bar on this side of town and ain't no hot blonde gonna do to him what he had done to him. Dead end. We got nothing."

"Well….he was an asshole anyway," the young cop shrugged as he turned the wheel and pulled the car out of the parking lot and into the street. "His own wife seemed relieved he was dead. Think she's the one that did it?"

"I'm telling you, kid, ain't NO woman did that to Eugene Walker…not a hot blonde and definitely not his fat ass wife! Drive!"

•••••••

The detective couldn't have been more wrong.

It was a hot blonde that took Eugene's life.

Exactly one week after he raped the girl outside the club she had been working in, Scarlet stalked Eugene Walker to a dive bar on the outskirts of town. She sat down next to him, struck up a conversation, coerced him off his barstool and right out the door.

It didn't take much coercion.

"It's Roni, right? You work at that whore club."

"Yes, sugar, that's me and that's exactly where I work," Scarlet let the words drip from her lips.

After a few shots of whiskey, they were headed into the woods behind the bar and after a few minutes in the woods, Scarlet was removing his belt.

"Love this huge buckle, baby. I noticed it in the bar," she spoke slowly and with purpose as she backed him against the tree.

"That's not all that's huge," he slurred.

Scarlet laughed, slipping the belt out of the last loop and positioning it so that the large buckle was dangling from her dominant hand. He made a move toward her and she grabbed the belt with her other hand so that she was holding it like a baseball bat.

She swung and the buckle crashed onto his face.

"What the…" he started but stumbled back as she swung again.

…and again.

…and again.

…and again.

His tooth flew out of his mouth and he fell hard against the tree, hitting his head and choking on the blood that was running down his face. He was making gargling noises in his throat.

Scarlet grabbed him by his feet and pulled so he was lying flat on his back and she brought the belt buckle down hard on his crotch.

He tried to scream but no noise could be heard through the blood erupting in his throat.

She brought the buckle of his own belt down on him again and again until he wasn't moving or making a sound. She threw the belt down, took a knife from her boot and with everything she had, plunged the knife into his chest and moved it slowly in a circle.

Scarlet leaned over his body, whispered something into his ear and then walked away, with the grace she was known to have.

...just as she had on the day, all those years ago, when she killed her father.

. . . .

Walker's blood hadn't even dried on Scarlet's skin when she drove out of the state of Tennessee. She crossed the state line of Kentucky and stopped at a fuel station. It was closed but it had an unlocked bathroom outside.

She pulled as close to the bathroom door as she could and stepped out of the car. Her jeans fit like a second skin. Her sleeveless white blouse - stained with blood - was unbuttoned halfway to her waist.

She cleaned up in the sink and changed her clothes. There was no river to watch her clothes float down this time, so she watched them burn in the garbage can instead.

Scarlet stood just outside the door, smoking a cigarette, and watching the reflection of the flames dancing on the white walls.

She closed her eyes expecting to relive her father's bloodbath, but she saw Vasco instead.

His inner light had been as lovely as his face. He had been so kind, generous and thoughtful. Scarlet was sure there were no more men like him in the world.

She remembered walking with him on the streets, hands as intertwined as their souls were. A smile stretched across her face every time she thought of him, but the smile faded when her mind strayed to the man that killed him.

Vasco had been stabbed while defending a woman on the street. A creole hooker they knew in passing was being slapped around so he stepped in to try to calm the situation. Vasco was unarmed and didn't stand a chance against the blade the pimp carried.

Scarlet wasn't there to help Vasco…and she had little luck getting help from the police after the attack.

…so, on her last trip to New Orleans, after she scattered Val's ashes, she paid the pimp a visit before she left.

The two men Scarlet beat to death – her father and Eugene Walker - had gotten off easily compared to what she had done to the man who took Vasco's life.

When the pimp's body was discovered, he had been bound, gagged, stabbed and mutilated. When they removed the gag, his missing dick was found in his throat.

Scarlet hadn't been sure which knife he had used to kill Vasco –he had so many lying around his apartment - so she poked holes in him with every single one of them.

Unlike the others, Scarlet talked to him the entire time, in her soothing voice. She told him why he deserved to die for his crimes against women and she told him all about Vasco.
.
"I'll see you in hell, you crazy bitch!" he yelled when he realized his pleas were pointless.

"Oh, sweetie," Scarlet said calmly as she stuck her finger in one of the knife holes, "we're already in hell."

He had cried and begged Scarlet for his life, but she had only smiled, looked into his eyes, stuffed his mouth and watched him choke on his own vomit.

Now, - just as then - she had no remorse as she watched the flames give way to smoke. Standing outside the bathroom of a gas station in the middle of nowhere, she felt just as free as she had when she ended her father's life.

Her father, the pimp, Eugene Walker…they all deserved exactly what they got, and she was happy to have been the one to give it to them.

…but she knew the satisfaction wouldn't last. For every man like Eugene Walker - for every man like her father - there were hundreds more just like them.

· · · · · · ·

She moved on after Walker; to a new look and a new place until she ran into more of the same and ended up covered in the blood of the wicked.

Time and again, the cycle repeated.

It became increasingly difficult for Scarlet to differentiate between the wickedness of men and the wickedness of **her**. She knew one day it would all come to an end…but it was too late to turn back. Scarlet decided to embrace who she was…and take out as many morally repugnant men as she could.

With each revenge killing, Scarlet felt like she had finally found (and embraced) a little more of herself. Her claws were out, and she was ready to take on any little mouse The Puppeteer sent her way.

Scarlet's growing acceptance of her murderous inclinations coincided with a shift of power in the strip clubs. In the mid-80s, rather than paying the girls to work, club owners began **charging** the girls to work. Stage fees, late fees and house fees put pressure on the dancers and became…in a lot of ways…

"Like having a pimp? Are you kidding me, Liz?"

"Exactly like having a pimp. I do the work and you stand there with your hand out," Scarlet answered.

Scarlet – or Liz as she was known at the time – had short black hair that feathered back on the sides. Her ocean eyes seared under her bangs. She wore a black bodysuit, black fishnet thigh-highs and a faux diamond arm cuff. Her red heels clicked across the hardwood floor as she crossed the room and placed her hand on the club owner's shoulder.

"We don't want any funny business here, Liz. NO SEX. We protect you from anyone even trying to…"

"Protection? Spoken like a true pimp, Mike," Scarlet interrupted.

"Look, Liz, I get it. I know you girls work hard but this is the new way," Mike tried to explain.

"Oh, I get it too, baby…but if I'm paying you, then you work for me. Not the other way around," she said, kissing his cheek and leaving a perfect red lip print.

"I'm pretty sure that's how it's always been anyway," Mike said.

"Great, then, as your boss, I have a special request. Mandy and I need the back room for an hour or so before we go out on the floor."

Mike raised his eyebrow.

"Yes…that's exactly why," she purred, licking her lips and winking at him.

"Can I watch?"

"No."

"Ugh…ok. You're the boss…but I need you girls on the floor in an hour!"

Mike had been doing this for a long time and women like Liz were a dying breed. She was sexy, smart and a hustler. It had been a long time since he had seen someone able to handle their drugs and their money as well as his star, Liz.

They don't make them like that anymore, he thought, adjusting himself as he watched her walk out the door.

......

As she embraced her power and her place in the game of life, Scarlet no longer waited to accidentally stumble across evil men.

She looked for them.

She hunted them.

They were never that hard to find…and stalking them became part of the fun. The watching and waiting were just as exciting as the killing. Gathering the necessary information, in order to be certain her mark deserved to die, ignited a fire inside her belly.

In the days before the internet, the library was the place to go for research. She could speed read through the slides on the microfilm machine and have a clear picture of who her target really was.

Scarlet loved the library. She loved the smell of the books, the quit stillness of the air and the sweet little librarians who always wanted to help.

She didn't have access to books as a child, so she devoured them as an adult. In the library, surrounded by endless knowledge and adventure, time would often slip away and she would find herself the last to leave at closing time.

"Did you find what you needed today, honey?" the little lady asked, pushing her large glasses up on the bridge of her nose. Her hair was gray and pulled into a tight bun at the base of her head.

"I did! I found exactly what I needed so I can complete my project," Scarlet said with a smile.

"I am so glad that we were able to help you, dear. You look like a woman who will do great things. Don't give up. It's a man's world out there…but that doesn't mean we can't still find our place in it."

"Thank you," Scarlet said. "I think I have finally found my place in this world of men."

"That's the spirit. Now, run along…and don't dally. It isn't safe after dark."

Indeed, it is not, Scarlet thought.

......

Chapter 6: Wicked Red

Her shiny black stiletto boots came just above her knee and her black leather mini hugged her hips. The sleeveless mock-neck body suit was, ironically, the color of fresh blood…as were her signature red lips and nails.

The bar was small and everything that wasn't already made of wood was the color of wood. The neon beer signs only lit up halfway and there was a faint smell of urine somewhere near.

Scarlet pushed another drink into his hand and finished up hers.

"You can call me Crystal," she purred.

"Is that your real name?" he slurred back at her.

"Nope."

"Ok, then…you can call me Al. What's a hot bitch like you doing in a shithole like this?"

Scarlet smiled and tucked his ratty hair behind his ear.

"Oh, I'm here for you, sugar. You and you alone. A very good friend told me about you…and if what she says is true, then this is going to be a night that I won't ever forget."

Born into hell and then suspended there – with no way of escape or salvation – Scarlet had finally found a way to thrive in the fiery chaos of her destiny.

......

Months later and hundreds of miles away, she walked down Miracle Mile to catch the trolley.

Scarlet wore high-waisted navy-blue shorts and a soft pink crop top. Her long hair was in a ponytail that bounced when she walked. Aviator sunglasses shielded her eyes from the sun and gave her a little anonymity on the busy street.

She would head to the Pink Pussycat later to dance and stock up some more cash, but she wanted to see a bit of the city first. She had never considered Miami as a destination until she had met two young women at the Palladium in New York.

Luna and Star were from Little Havana. Star, the taller of the two, had thick black hair, golden-brown skin and a tight ass that men went crazy for. Her laugh was infectious, and she and Scarlet hit it off right away. Luna was younger than Star with skin like caramel silk and tawny eyes beneath long, dark lashes.

The three of them worked the men in the club for money, booze and drugs and then met in a hotel room to party into the early morning hours.

"You have to go to Miami," Star said, laying out a line of coke.

"The men are so easy there," Luna added.

Scarlet snorted her line off the mirror and sat back against the pillows that were piled up against the headboard.

"They are pretty easy everywhere," Star continued, "I meant the city. The heat, the food…and yes, the men, but the city itself is a non-stop party."

"How do you decide where to go next?" Luna asked, adjusting the strap on her lowcut dress.

"Depends on what I need at the time. Sometimes I go where the money is and sometimes, I go to small towns when I want to slow down and rest up a bit."

"I never want to slow down," Star smiled.

Scarlet poured three more shots and Star laid out three more lines.

"Tonight, I don't want to either," Scarlet winked.

. . . . . .

"Bitch! You came!" Luna squealed when she saw Scarlet enter the dressing room of the Pink Pussycat in Miami.

Star jumped up with one eyelash on and hugged Scarlet tight.

It was nice to see some familiar faces. Scarlet had been on her own for so long, she had forgotten what that was like.

"I told you I would come," Scarlet smiled.

"Yeah but that was like six months ago," Luna said, finishing up her lipstick. "We gave up on you."

"We are going to have a fucking blast! How long are you staying?" Star asked.

"I'm not sure yet," Scarlet answered placing her bag in the chair between the two girls.

"I hope it will be for a while," a man's voice said behind them.

Star and Luna ran over to hug the Pussycat's manager, Hal.

"You brought in a real doll, this time, girls," Hal said returning the hugs.

Hal looked like he was straight out of a mobster movie, pinky rings and all. As were most of the club managers where Scarlet worked, he was a nice guy and good to the girls.

"You haven't seen anything yet, baby," Scarlet answered.

......

"How in the holy fuck do you get me into these situations, Star?" Luna asked dryly, standing naked over the fully clothed body of a middle-aged man.

"You guys have done this before?" Scarlet asked, surprised.

"It happens a lot, honestly," Star said.

"So, what are we supposed to do now?" Scarlet asked.

"He'll be out cold for a few hours. We take everything. He was going to give it all to us before the night was over anyway."

"Then we just...leave him here? Won't he call the police when he wakes up?" Scarlet asked.

"And say what? That he met three women at a bar, did too many drugs, passed out and got robbed...in his own hotel room?"

Luna took off his watch and Star cleaned out his pockets.

Scarlet was noticeably uncomfortable stealing.

Star explained, "fuck this guy, all the ones before him and all the ones that will come after, girl. They don't play fair, why the fuck should we?"

...and in that moment, Scarlet realized that her own set of morals, while questionable, weren't flexible.

Everyone is playing the same game...but how we choose to move the pieces makes all the difference.

....

The street was dark and empty, except for the two of them.

Scarlet wore a ribbed mini dress, that showed off her curves and her long legs. It was blue with a scoop neck and short sleeves. Her hoop earrings were silver, and the matching necklace sparkled when the light hit it. Her bangles clinked together when she moved her hands...and she was always moving her hands. Her blue and black heels clicked against the pavement and her hips swayed with every step.

"I'm a good judge of people…and you look like the kind of woman that eats her steak rare," he said.

"Well, super-sleuth, I'm a vegetarian," Scarlet answered. "I haven't eaten meat since I was a little girl."

"Humans were made to eat meat. I got some meat I think you'll like," he snarled, grabbing his crotch.

"You want me to rip that apart with my teeth?" Scarlet asked, motioning to his crotch and becoming much more interested.

"If you can fit it all in your mouth…"

"I'd much rather see if we can fit it into yours," Scarlet interrupted narrowing her eyes.

He stepped toward her and she struck quickly with 3 stabs to his side and one to his gut.

. . . .

Scarlet arched her back against the pole and looked seductively to the side at the man on her right.

He was holding a dollar…in his mouth.

Gross, she thought, but she kept her face neutral.

She leaned against the pole, slid down to a seated position with one leg extended. She extended her other leg, crossed her ankles and put them behind her head.

She slowly let one leg float down and then the other, arching her back. She rolled over and pushed onto all fours, gliding like a lioness on the prowl.

She never broke eye contact and made sure she moved as slowly as she could, allowing him to become as uncomfortable as possible.

A crowd had gathered around the stage, but Scarlet's only focus was on the man with the dollar in his mouth. Once she reached him, she looked deeper into his eyes and then yanked the dollar out of his lips with her hand.

The men around the stage laughed.

Scarlet winked.

...then she turned her focus to the next...and the next. Once she had made her way around to all the customers at the stage, she stood up to go back to the pole.

There was some commotion so Scarlet turned around to see a drunk man trying to climb up onto the stage. She looked for the bouncer, but he was busy hitting on one of the girls. Annoyed, Scarlet handled it herself.

She walked casually to the edge of the stage, put the forefront of her stone-studded boot on his forehead and pushed him backward, away from the stage.

He stumbled and then fell over a table and into the floor.

She gathered her money and her money bag and walked off the stage in the middle of her set. This wasn't the first time Scarlet had to handle a situation herself…and it pissed her off every time.

The manager was waiting for her when she got off stage.

"I'm sorry but you have to finish your set, Jackie", he said, uncomfortable.

"You and the bouncer can finish my set and then after, you can go fuck yourselves," Scarlet responded.

He followed her to the dressing room still trying to assert some sort of dominance. Scarlet opened her locker, blocking his face from her view and took out her bag, throwing the strap over her shoulder. She reached inside, took out some money, and closed the locker door.

She sprinkled her tip-out money on his feet and then walked out the back door, triggering the automatic alarm.

"Ok, but you're coming back tomorrow, right?" he called after her. "We need girls like you," he yelled over the alarm.

Scarlet, kept walking, flicked him off with both of her middle fingers and never looked back.

• • • • • •

She moved across the stage with a slow rhythm that was seductive and enchanting. No matter which city she worked in, no one had ever seen anyone dance like Scarlet. Everything from top to bottom was sculpted through the eyes of pure desire. She oozed sex appeal from the fibers of her very being.

She could change her hair color and her name over and over, but she could never change the unadulterated magic of her movements.

When she wasn't hypnotizing men with her body, she was confounding them with her intelligence, charm and wit...because to find a woman both gorgeous and smart was perplexing to the male gender.

"She's a little intimidating...that one over there. The redhead. Have you ever talked to her?"

"Nah. She looks like a bitch."

"She's actually pretty nice...and she's funny. I don't know...there is something different about her."

"There is something different about all of them. Isn't that why we come here? For variety! Otherwise we could just stay home with our wives, right?"

The shorter of the two men laughed and slapped his buddy on the back as he asked the question. The taller man shrugged it off and gave a half-hearted laugh but stopped short when he made eye contact with the redhead exiting the stage. Her eyes burned through his and suddenly his pants felt a little tighter.

"That's not what I mean, Joe. I mean, she's special. They broke the mold when they made that one," he said not daring to lose sight of her eyes or her favor.

Joe laughed again and replied, "Just go on and hand her your wallet, Chuck. Hell, give her your keys too. You are getting fucked tonight and not in a good way, my friend. That's not the kind of woman that puts out in a place like this. You'll be working harder than she will tonight."

Joe was right.

Chuck did not get to physically fuck, but he was absolutely mind-fucked that night by the redhead who called herself Vixen.

BOOK TWO

"Look at me!

You don't look so good, Armani. You are fading in and out a little. "Poor Fucked Chuck", you are probably thinking, that guy didn't deserve to lose all his money chasing a dream of pussy he couldn't have, but don't forget...these men came into the clubs looking for ME. I wasn't chasing them down in the streets or enticing them to hand over their cash in front of their church on Sundays.

Stay with me!

Keep your eyes open, for fucks sake. Did I really 'take advantage' of **them** when they entered the building with their dicks in their hands thinking that **they** would be taking advantage of **me**? They willingly handed over their earnings in the hopes that it would buy them a touch or a taste. So, I left with all their money and they left with blue balls...could have been worse, right?

Open your eyes!

Dammit, Armani, I feel like you aren't paying attention. Here, do this bump....there you go...that's better...

Do you see me?

All the drugs can really fuck with your vision. You've had quite the candy box collection of party favors tonight! For all the shit you guys talk, I've found that few of you are really capable of hanging with me when it comes to getting fucked up...or having a conversation...or...come to think of it, where the hell did all the 'male superiority' bullshit come from? Take away your dick and what do you have that I don't?

Calm down!

I wasn't implying that I was going to take your dick. Don't be so paranoid. Just because I cut off a few in my time doesn't mean I just go around collecting them. What would I do with a bag of dicks?

What I'm saying is being a woman is harder than being a man. We have to do everything you do but we get paid less for doing it. We endure your sexist attitudes from birth. You rape our sisters and our daughters then teach your sons to do the same by **not** teaching them **not** to fucking do it.

It is a war zone for women out there and it begins for us when we are still little girls. I was simply a survivor fighting a war I didn't start because I was born into a life I couldn't escape.

...and in war, it's an eye for an eye, baby.

...or I guess in this case, a dick for a dick.

Right, Armani?"

Chapter 1: Divine Decree

The clubs provided the perfect cover and the perfect diversion. Scarlet moved in and out of them as she pleased. She gathered information quickly and discreetly.

When she wanted to rest, she rested.

When she wanted to hunt, she hunted.

All the while, stacking money on top of money to pay for whatever she needed or wanted for her quests.

The people that owned, operated and worked in the clubs had their own sub-culture and their own lingo. Every night was a party and the girls had access to whatever they wanted: drugs, alcohol, food, men and sex.

Most nights, the dressing room was like a big dress up party with girls doing each other's makeup and sharing outfits. There was a lot of gossip and a lot of laughter.

On bad days, there were screaming matches, cat fights and inevitably ended with someone drunk and crying in the corner.

Scarlet was there for the money…but she occasionally dabbled in the rest. If she was going to work in a non-stop party, she figured she might as well enjoy the party favors.

......

Life in the clubs passed quickly for Scarlet. After a decade, she saw fashion circle back in on itself and music go through stages and changes.

The club owners began to see the girls as valuable and therefore began to treat them as such. The ones that didn't know, learned quickly when Scarlet passed through.

She not only reminded the managers and owners of the importance of taking care of the workers responsible for padding their pockets, she constantly mentored the women she met and reminded them of their own individual worth.

"The Girls" - as the dancers were referred to - were pretty much the same in every city back then. Before human traffickers took over, The Girls were there by and of their own choice and every club was made up of:

Single Mothers,

College Students,

one Super Freak (just there for the thrill),

a few Drug Addicts (supporting expensive habits),

a Prostitute (in disguise as a stripper),

someone with Daddy Issues (her customers have gray hair),

The Outcast (usually mentally unstable)

…and of course, The Hustlers.

The Hustlers could make it in any arena. In another life, they could be hard-core business professionals of any industry. They show up on time, are self-motivated and they don't take 'no' for an answer. Their stacks of cash are fat, and their tongues are made of silver.

Every girl at every club fell into one of these categories. Some of them might fit neatly into two or even three, but there was always one that fit them best.

Scarlet was a hustler and one of the best anyone had ever seen in those days. She usually worked by herself, she never got caught up in drama and she made men pay her for her time. She made everything look effortless.

She was enjoying some downtime at a small club in the middle of nowhere. You could practically see the back of the club from the front door. There were pool tables on either side of the entrance.

Scarlet hated pool tables inside the clubs. They were a waste of space and invited men with empty pockets to waste space alongside them.

"How does she make so much money? I never see her take her clothes off and she hardly ever dances," whined Daddy Issues.

.

"Right? She just sits around talking and getting fucked up all night and leaves with a pile of cash, but have you seen her on stage? I've never seen anyone dance like that. She looks like a cross between a snake and a cat," replied Super Freak.

"That's a helluva combo."

Super Freak moistened her lips before she replied, "exactly."

"Yeah, I guess I can see it. If I was a guy, she would definitely give me a tickle in my pickle."

"I don't have a pickle and I've got a tickle…in my vagina."

"Ew," Daddy Issues laughed and continued, "don't say 'vagina'…"

"Ok, then…a…fever in my beaver?"

Both girls laughed until they heard a voice behind them. Their eyes widened and they stopped abruptly, spinning around in their chairs.

"Thank you, doll, never heard that one before. Let me buy you a drink," Scarlet motioned for a waitress as she spoke.

She turned her green eyes coolly at Daddy Issues, letting her know it was time for her to vacate. When she was gone, Scarlet took her chair.

"I'm sorry, um…." Super Freak stumbled over her words caught in the captivating gaze of the woman in front of her.

"Ava," Scarlet replied, pushing her long, dark hair over her shoulder. "My name is Ava."

"My name…."

"That's ok, baby," Scarlet leaned in and placed her hand on Super Freak's thigh, "I don't need to know your name. I just want to hear about your fever."

Minutes later, with drinks in hand, they disappeared to the back of the club with all eyes on them. Imaginations ran wild, but no one in the club was creative enough to picture what happened between the two.

. . . .

The lights blurred around the edges, a sign that the buzz would soon kick in.

She felt a lazy smile creep across her face, and she felt like a thousand butterflies were dancing in her belly. She leaned back in her chair and stretched her arms high above her head. The sound of her bracelets bumping into one another, falling down her wrist sounded like tiny bells. She brought her arms back down, rested her hands in her lap, uncrossed her legs and then crossed them the other way.

Every movement, every sound brought feelings of joy and ecstasy.

What a great time to be alive, she thought. *What a perfect place to be, right here, right now.*

Scarlet closed her eyes and let the entire world wash over her. It lapped at her skin. It flowed through her hair. It bathed her soul. This was a ride in the clouds she never wanted to come down from.

"When you are done with your nap, could you please sit with some of the customers, Nadia?" he asked in a fake polite voice that was half-joking.

Scarlet opened her eyes slowly and answered, "I'm waiting for them to come to me."

"Yeah…that's not going to happen. Look at you. You are intimidating, as hell, Nadia. I didn't even want to come over here to ask you to work…and I'm your boss."

Scarlet stood, put her hands on either side of his face, looked into his eyes and smiled. When she sauntered away to the bar, he watched her shaking his head in disbelief. Girls like Nadia were few and far between in the industry. She was a major pain in his ass but damn, did she bring in the money.

One of the nicer clubs in the area, The Mousetrap was known for its high-end girls. The upscale décor and overpriced drinks were aimed at a specific clientele. The walls were all mirrors and rich purple fabrics covered the chairs and barstools.

Above the bar, a line of purple pendant lights hung low and in between songs, the faint sound of glasses clinking could be heard in the distance. There were stages at either end of the club with tables and chairs in between and it was a packed house every night.

The bartender's skirt was short. Her purple and black bustier pushed her tits up and out. She wore back fishnet thigh-high stockings and heeled black boots. Scarlet winked at her.

Scarlet chose to approach two suits at the bar first. Suits were her favorite. They were often arrogant, and she reveled in watching them suffer. The men wearing suits had a need to prove themselves and always shelled out a lot of dough to compensate for their other shortcomings.

She delicately placed a hand on each of their backs and said, "so, what are we drinking tonight, fellas?"

They turned in their seats, the one on her left making eye contact first and with a drawl that sounded like home, he exclaimed, "well, I'll be a monkey's uncle! Scarlet?"

Recognition crashed over her and though she normally kept a respectable demeanor under any circumstance, she leapt into his arms. They embraced with the enthusiasm of those who've been separated by time and distance for so long that reuniting seemed impossible.

Scarlet beamed as she pulled back to look at his face. He looked older. There were a few gray hairs just above his ears and he had a crease in his brow, but Leo's smile hadn't changed, at all.

"Dammit, girl…how do you look like you've hardly aged since I dropped you off in N'Awlins?"

"This pasty-ass complexion turned out to be a bit of a blessing-in-disguise. I can't bake in the sun like these beautiful bronze bitches, but in turn I get to look younger than I am," Scarlet replied, still smiling like an excited kid.

"Where'd your accent go?" he asked, still amazed to see her there.

"Oh, it's still here when I want it to be, sugah," she answered in an exaggerated southern accent.

Leo laughed.

"Atta, girl! What's it been, Scarlet? How many years? Let's get some drinks and catch up! This is my partner, Ezra. Ezra this is Scarlet."

"Actually, in here, I go by 'Nadia'. I like to keep my anonymity," she replied with a wink.

Scarlet turned her attention to meet Ezra and found herself briefly speechless. Tall, with dark skin and light brown eyes…he was a gorgeous man. She would know this man for more than one night…of this she was certain.

He seemed to be equally as infatuated with Scarlet as he stood to take her hand. A knowing smile was pulling at the sides of his full lips. He pulled her hand to his mouth and kissed it slowly, never breaking eye contact.

Leo looked from one to the other and said playfully, "easy now."

"You said partners?" Scarlet asked not taking her eyes away from Ezra's.

"Yes, ma'am," Leo answered as he motioned to the bartender to give them a round. "We work for the government. Special unit. In town doing some research."

"Cold cases," Ezra added. His voice was deep and sexy, but his response snapped Scarlet back to reality instantly.

"That sounds exciting," she said looking from one to the other. "Like murder?"

"Yes," Leo answered, "but you don't want to hear about that. Tell me what you've been doing! I want every detail."

Well played, Puppet Master, Scarlet thought. *You dirty, deranged bastard…well fucking played.*

·······

The elderly couple Scarlet was renting from were two of the first people she had met when she arrived in Marietta, GA. They approached her at a diner and said she reminded them of the granddaughter they lost in a car accident several years prior.

When they found out that Scarlet was new in town, they excitedly told her they had recently listed the apartment above their garage for rent and insisted she look at it.

Scarlet loved it immediately. The apartment was built above a detached 4-car garage, so it was spacious enough for her needs. It had a studio-style layout and was already furnished.

All the walls were painted the same color. In the living area, there was a red sofa and matching chair with a contemporary rug and coffee table that faced a television. The kitchenette had linoleum flooring, tile countertops and small appliances. There were pots, pans, dishes…everything Scarlet needed.

Behind the pony wall was a queen size bed with a wrought iron headboard. Hanging above it was a painting of a woman with a red umbrella. Opposite the bed was a long chest of drawers and next to it a small closet which contained a washer and dryer.

The bathroom had the same linoleum as the kitchen with a clawfoot tub in the center.

The drive and entrance were far enough from the main house that Scarlet didn't have to worry about disturbing anyone with her late hours and they said she could use the pool whenever she liked.

It was perfect for her.

"God works in mysterious ways," the sweet lady had said with her hazel eyes sparkling.

As Scarlet stared at the ceiling, reeling with the past week's events, she recalled her first meeting with her landlords and remembered those words:

God works in mysterious ways.

"Indeed, he does," she said aloud.

She sat up and took her pipe from her pocket, loaded it and watched the green turn orange in the bowl as she held the fire from her lighter above it. She inhaled deeply and relaxed her breath out slowly, watching the smoke coil in circles around her.

Her mind settled on Leo and Ezra.

She had spent time with them every day over the week following their accidental meeting at the club. They had lunch the first day and dinner the following evening. They went out for drinks, attended a concert and learned a lot about each other.

Leo didn't talk much about work, but in the moments she spent alone with him, Ezra chattered on about a possible serial killer and new DNA testing.

Leo had a wife. He had a picture of her in his wallet that he showed off proudly and he told Scarlet all about her. She told them about her time in New Orleans with Vasco and Val and made them laugh with her intellectual wit.

"I think you are in the wrong profession," Leo had said as he lit her cigarette. "You are too fucking smart to be…"

"…taking money from the innocent?" she finished, daring him to challenge her.

This wasn't the first time someone had approached her with a similar line. She had many comebacks on hand.

…making more money than you?

…taking advantage of men who are trying to take advantage of women?

…utilizing my looks in a society that focuses entirely on the importance of them?

"Nah, kiddo. They aren't that innocent. It's just…a lot of those women are there because they have to be. You don't have to."

"Few of us are there because we have to be. The majority of us are there because we want to be. We have different reasons…different paths that brought us there, but at the end of the day, we make our own choices. I know a different side of that world than the one that can be seen looking in from your perspective."

"Now calm down, darlin', I didn't mean to offend, and you are absolutely right. You do have an insider's perspective," he spoke in a soothing voice and motioned for the bartender to keep them coming. "You actually might be able to give us some insight into our investigation."

Scarlet kept her face calm and cool just as she always did. Her movements were slow and planned, but inside, her chest tightened.

She pulled all her hair around to one side and winked as she took a long, slow drag from her cigarette. After watching the smoke for a moment, she leaned in and said, "I thought you'd never ask. What do you want to know?"

"Something you said the first night…about anonymity. The girls don't give real names, so is it likely the customers don't either?" Leo asked.

"Sure. Some of them use aliases. Especially the married ones. Why?"

Leo paused deciding what he should divulge and what he shouldn't before answering.

"A few of these cold cases involve men whose last known whereabouts were strip clubs. It was hard to get straightforward information back then and even harder now. The turnover at these clubs is crazy and with all the fake names and everyone drinking…"

Scarlet relaxed from the inside out, took a breath and said, "Sounds impossible."

Leo gave her his boyish grin and a wink.

"Nothing's impossible, darlin'."

Sitting in her apartment, smoking her bowl and watching the circles of smoke dissipate, Scarlet recounted her conversation with Leo.

God works in mysterious ways and nothing is impossible, she thought.

A knock at the door sent her skidding back from her daydream.

Chapter 2: The Beaten, the Broken and the Damned

She opened the door to Ezra and watched in mild panic as the smoke rolled out the door and right into his face. She looked past him for Leo and was relieved when she didn't see him.

"He's not with me," Ezra smiled playfully at her. "Did I, um, interrupt something?"

"No. Come inside. I was just…I don't inhale," she showed a smile in her eyes but none on her face. It was one of her many talents.

"Oh, so you follow politics?"

"Why do you sound surprised?"

"Nothing about you surprises me, Scarlet. You are…"

"…stellar? Stupendous?" She offered when he couldn't find the words to finish.

He smiled and stepped closer to her, searching her eyes before he said, "you are an extraordinary woman, Scarlet, I mean really **extraordinary**…and I am…I am a very ordinary man."

…but Ezra **was** an extraordinary man. He was six foot, three inches and two hundred and forty pounds of extraordinary man. His eyes sparkled and his full lips were inviting. He had big hands and Scarlet was certain he could do some extraordinary things with those fingers.

"You aren't ordinary, baby," Scarlet said in her slow, sexy way.

"Are you saying what I think you're saying?" Ezra asked, stepping toward her.

Scarlet looked deeply into his eyes and after a moment answered, "sorry, I'm really high. Are we talking about fucking? Because....yes. I want to do that."

He laughed and pulled her into him covering his mouth with hers. They kissed slowly, at first but then more intensely. He picked her up with ease and she wrapped her legs around his waist.

He carried her over to her bed, never taking his mouth off hers and sat down on the edge. They continued this way, sweetly but the sweetness eventually gave way to savagery.

Ezra tore at her clothes and she at his.

When he had her topless, he ran his wide tongue over her nipple and then slowly around it in a circle before taking all of her into his mouth.

His skin was soft, but his touch was just rough enough to excite Scarlet in all the right places.

....

Ezra laid opposite Scarlet looking into her eyes. He wondered how many men had been lucky enough to know this pleasure...to look at this beautiful woman from this position...but he didn't dare ask.

"Your face is pretty, "Scarlet said.

Ezra laughed.

"Pretty? I don't get that one often…actually…never."

"Are you more comfortable with the word 'lovely'? You are a very lovely man, Ezra. Nothing wrong with that. You have nice, soft skin," she said, touching his face.

"I'm pretty comfortable with whatever you call me, as long as you're calling me," he answered, closing his hand around hers.

Scarlet smiled and bit her bottom lip.

"I'd like to…call you, if that's ok. I'd like to do this again, Ezra."

"I'll have to check my schedule…"

"Seriously," Scarlet asked playfully, sitting up.

"Something tells me that you aren't used to hearing the word 'no'…and we both know I won't be the one to say it to you," Ezra smiled, pulling her on top of him. "You've got me hooked, girl. You can call me whenever and whatever you like. I'll come running."

Scarlet adjusted her hips, positioning him between her legs and he grabbed her ass with both hands.

"I don't need you to come running, baby. I just need you to come."

……

The next night, she dreamed of Vasco. The smell of his skin, the taste of his mouth lingered even after she woke and wiped the tears from her face. Her dreams of him had been fewer and farther between until she had connected with Ezra. Now, it seemed that she dreamed of Vasco every night.

Ezra would never be to her what Vasco was.

No one would.

You only get that kind of love once in a lifetime.

Scarlet sat up, pulled her pillow into her stomach and rocked back and forth. It soothed her, just as it had when she was a little girl.

When she was young, her father would often offer her body to his friends in exchange for money. After a while, she got tired of fighting them. She would just lay there, trying to go somewhere else in her mind. Once they left the room, she would hold her pillow and rock until the pain subsided.

The physical pain wasn't the worst part. She got used to that after a while. The worst part was the pain that ached deep inside her soul beneath everything else. A pain she couldn't touch or soothe.

It was the pain of knowing that no one was coming to save her.

It was the pain of loneliness and betrayal.

So, she would do the only thing she could. Rock herself. Repeat the movements, back and forth…back and forth until the tears stopped and her internal pain disappeared with them.

. . . .

"I found a place that's supposed to have some great vegetarian dishes," Ezra told Scarlet through the closed door.

"Sounds good, honey, but you know I always figure it out, either way," she replied while entering the room.

Her long sleeve, black top pushed her tits up high and brought attention to her narrow waist. Her black and red plaid skirt was short and tight. Her heeled boots, also black, came to her knee.

Her hair was down, the sparkle of her hoops hidden until she moved a certain way. Her lips and nails were red...her favorite color.

"Wow," was all Ezra could say.

He was wearing black dress pants and a long sleeve shirt in a dark-colored paisley print.

"Right backatcha, sexy," Scarlet replied, stepping toward him.

"Ok...ok...you two have time for that later," Leo called from the couch.

Scarlet and Ezra broke eye contact and joined him in the living area of Scarlet's apartment. They were laughing and headed for the door when the phone rang.

"You said I could call if I ever needed you," the voice said on the line.

"Ally? Yes, of course, honey. What's wrong? Are you ok?"

"I think so. I feel kind of stupid calling, actually."

"No problem. What's going on?"

"My landlord sent this guy over...and I don't know. He's just kind of giving me the creeps."

"Do you need me to come over?"

"No...no...maybe just stay on the line with me?"

"Absolutely, little sister! Is he inside with you right now?"

"No...he stepped out to check a pipe or something outside."

"Ok...when he comes back in, start talking to me about your boyfriend. Say he will be by to pick you up soon. Doesn't matter that you don't have one. Mention your Dad living nearby...a brother...as many people as you can so he knows you aren't alone, and people will be checking on you."

Leo and Ezra, only able to hear Scarlet's side of the conversation, exchanged glances.

"Girl, there's all kinds of things you can do if that doesn't work. You can make him think you're crazy as hell...so he will be the one afraid of you.

You can get in a fight with a lamp.

Let the lamp win.

You can strap your vibrator to your leg and run at him – with it bouncing side-to-side yelling 'HEY! YOU WANT TO PLAY A GAME?'

The main thing is just stay calm and stay on the phone with me until he's gone," Scarlet said.

When she hung up the phone, Leo and Ezra were staring.

"What?" Scarlet asked.

"What the fuck was that?" Ezra asked.

"Nice world you guys live in where the handyman isn't going to attack you, huh? Where you can let strangers in to fix your pipes and not have to worry about protecting your literal ass from them and their…pipes?"

"We are all living in the same world, aren't we?…and not all men are rapists," Ezra replied.

Scarlet laughed.

"We are **not** living in the same world. Women have to stay on guard, and we have to look out for each other. It is the difference between life and death for us. I would think that you two – being in the field you are in – would understand that more than most men."

"I get it," Leo said.

"I mean, yeah...I suppose I do too," Ezra added.

"Obviously, suggesting she get in a fight with the furniture was a joke...a way to make her laugh to calm her...but the rest? That's how it must be done. If they know you live alone or don't have any family or friends...then you become a bigger target. Big military boyfriend...big brother...let them think there's a big man of some kind coming to check up on you."

"So, is that what you tell people?" Ezra asked, mostly to stroke his own ego.

"No," Scarlet replied. "I have a different approach to remind men why they shouldn't fuck with me."

......

Scarlet and Ezra had spoken on the phone every day since he left to go back to his home in Virginia. He was planning on flying down to see her again in a few weeks.

She had just hung the phone up in the cradle when it rang again. She thought he had forgotten to tell her something, so she answered, "miss me already?"

"I fucked up, girl. I need help," her longtime friend, Ryin's voice sounded steady but concerned.

"Ok. Calm down, honey. Where are you?" Scarlet asked.

"I'm in Fuck-It-All, Alabama...at my dad's house. Pretty sure I just killed the mother fucker. I'm going to have to turn myself in," her voice broke on the last word.

"The hell you will. I'll be there in three hours. Don't move."

Scarlet felt like the drive to Ryin's hometown took twice as long as it should have. It was only her second time driving there and the first time, Ryin had been with her and they were driving from a different direction. She had plenty of time to think about her best friend and the only person she had been close to since Val died.

Ryin was an ebony goddess with an amazing body and a humor that matched Scarlet's. Underneath her perfectly sculpted eyebrows, her lids were always swept with just a touch of gold powder. Long lashes, with milk chocolate eyes were framed by a smooth, short hairstyle-inspired by a popular actress of the time. Her high cheekbones, broad nose, plump lips and perfect teeth made her a truly stunning woman.

They met while working at a club in Ft Lauderdale and had become friends right away. Their souls reached out to one another, past the outward beauty and into the plummeting depths of their childhood pain. There, somewhere inside, they pictured themselves as two little girls clinging on with no one else in the world but each other.

One night after work, when Ryin trusted her enough, she shared her story with Scarlet.

"He raped me for eight years. It started when I was six years old. What kind of sick fuck looks at a six-year-old....you know what? I can't. I can't talk about it. I'm thirty fucking years old and I still can't talk about it....and don't tell anybody, ok?" Ryin pushed back tears as she rolled a hundred-dollar bill into a straw.

"About your dad? I would never," Scarlet answered with true compassion.

"No...that I'm thirty years old," she answered, shaking off the feelings that tried to creep in.

Scarlet looked at her knowingly and offered a wink.

"I would definitely never tell anyone that...and they wouldn't believe me anyway."

She snorted a line from the mirror with the cash straw Ryin handed her and continued, "fuck your piece of shit father, honey. Men like that always get what they deserve."

"He doesn't seem to. After my mother died, he moved someone else in right away...Sam...Pam...I don't remember her fucking name. Fuck them both sideways. I was out there struggling just trying to feel normal and they are sitting up in my mother's house...uh-uh. I can't, girl. I can't."

"We could tie them up and set the house on fire with them in it," Scarlet's eyes widened as she spoke.

Ryin laughed, "you're so fucking crazy, girl! That's why you're my bestie. I don't know what I'd do without you."

Ryin had no way of knowing that Scarlet was serious. Scarlet only shared a little of her childhood story with Ryin. She told her of the physical abuse, but not of the rapes. She felt that what happened to Ryin was far worse because it was her own father that tore her innocence away from her.

They would often talk long into the night, over drinks, about the strength of rebuilding after the storm of domestic violence pulls the walls down around you...but Scarlet never trusted Ryin enough to speak about the demons that were born from the storm.

She never trusted anyone with her demons.

Everyone has demons. Some are small and convince you to take the last piece of cake. Some are bigger and convince you to lie and cheat. Some demons, like Scarlet's, can gobble up human life with no remorse. The scariest part isn't that we all have demons. It's that those 'demons' are just primitive thoughts of our own design.

There is no horned devil hiding in the shadows controlling them.

We control them ourselves and Scarlet's demons would always be her own secret playthings that roared inside her head and took away her pain.

....

Scarlet arrived in the sleepy town they'd nicknamed 'Fuck-It-All" and found the drive that was lined on either side with crepe myrtles. She turned right with her high beams blazing.

At the end of the long driveway, partially hidden by two large oak trees, she saw the house.

Even in the dark, it was an impressive estate. The red brick mini mansion was surrounded by vibrant flowers. An American flag waved in the breeze. The Colonel's home looked so warm and inviting, but Scarlet knew the dark secrets within.

The porchlight was on and Ryin was on the front steps. Scarlet parked in front of the steps, got out of the car and sat down next to her friend. Ryin's eyes were puffy and Scarlet knew she was on the brink of cracking like broken glass under pressure.

"What happened?"

"I pushed his old ass down the stairs. He's lying in there on the last step with his bones poking through his skin. I'm going to jail, sister. They are going to lock me up and throw away the key."

"He's dead?"

"I wish he would fucking die. He's still alive. Going on and on about him being an officer in the military and me being a whore and when the police get here...."

"Has he called the police?"

"No. He can't get to the phone. It's in the kitchen and he's too drunk to drag himself in there. I hate him. He stole my childhood from me. He made me grow up feeling used and ashamed. I found out while I was here for the funeral for Sam...Pam...whatever the fuck her name was, he did the same thing to my nieces that he did to me."

"I'm so sorry, Ryin. He's a piece of shit. Did you want him to die when you pushed him?"

"Yes, Scarlet. Of course, I did. I wanted that child rapist to burn in fucking hell."

"Does he smoke cigars, by chance?"

Ryin nodded.

"He's going to burn, baby girl. He's going to burn tonight."

·······

Scarlet tried to talk Ryin into leaving for Atlanta while she stayed behind to take care of things, but Ryin insisted on staying to see it through to the end.

They packed some - but not all of Ryin's things - and put them in Ryin's car.

"You are going to say that you called me to tell me about your trip and I was very upset about my boyfriend cheating on me. So, you spoke with your dad and he said he would be fine if you drove up to spend the night with me," Scarlet instructed.

Scarlet laid out the plan with an eerie calm as she inspected the cigars.

"Then, you, sir," she said, holding his chin up to pour more alcohol into his mouth, "tripped your drunk ass right down the stairs while holding a lit cigar and set yourself on fire. What a clumsy dumbass, you are," she finished, dropping his face on the floor.

He mumbled profanities under his breath.

"Now, now, you disgusting douchehole, that's no way to talk to a lady. Don't make me shove this bottle up your ass," Scarlet said as she forced more alcohol down his throat.

Both Ryin and Scarlet stopped for a moment, pondering if the idea was possible, but got back to work on the plan.

After they made sure everything was in place, they went to work on the biggest bonfire Fuck-It-All, Alabama would see for quite some time. It took several tries to get his pajamas to catch, but after they figured out that leaving the Zippo open in his breast pocket would speed it along, the flames took hold and the fire began to eat him alive.

He screamed.

He cried.

He begged.

His begging is what finally shattered the rest of the broken glass inside Ryin's delicate mind.

"Begging, you fucking **bastard**? Are you begging *me*? I begged **you** to stop, you son-of-a-bitch!" Ryin yelled. "I was a little girl! A helpless baby girl," she sobbed through her screams and dropped to her knees in front of him to be closer to his face.

His skin bubbled and his screams became wilder. The stench of burning flesh rose with the smoke in the air. Scarlet looked around the grand entry of the estate to estimate how much time they had.

It really was such a beautiful place. It was a true shame that it would soon be nothing more than a pile of ashes and charred remnants of what once was.

She had always imagined that people who lived in houses like this didn't have the same kinds of problems that people like her did, but the more people she met, the more she realized, dysfunction doesn't care about your social class.

It doesn't care about your race.

It doesn't care about your religion, your finances or your gender.

Dysfunction is a monster that can be bred in any home, Scarlet thought, looking back at her friend.

"Look at me! How does **that** feel, Colonel? Fire burning through your skin and you can't move? You can't fight it? You just have to lay there and TAKE IT?" Ryin gritted her teeth and tears streamed down her face.

Scarlet pulled her back as the flames engulfed his face and guided her toward the front door saying, "come on, honey. I need you to get in your car. This house is massive, but it won't take long to burn. Remember what I told you."

Ryin took a deep breath as they reached the fresh air outside. When she calmed herself enough, she said robotically, "I'm going to follow you in my car. We're driving to your apartment. Do not speed and do not stop anywhere."

"Yes. Perfect," Scarlet soothed. "He will never hurt another little girl again, Ryin. It's over, baby."

·······

Beyond their early morning discussion when they arrived safely home, Ryin and Scarlet never spoke of what happened to the Colonel again.

They held hands at his funeral while people spoke half-heartedly about his accomplishments.

He wasn't kind. He wasn't generous. He was mean and told jokes that made women uncomfortable. He drank too much, and he hurt innocent children. There was a strange, unspoken whisper through the eyes and actions of those in attendance that the old man had gotten what he deserved.

No one said that aloud, of course....not in America....and damn sure not in the south.

Imagine if people stood up at funerals and shared their true feelings about the departed:

"He fought proudly for his country...and he also beat his wife. I'm so glad he died before he killed her in front of her children."

"She sang like an angel...and was an ignorant racist. I'm really glad she's not around anymore so I can love who I want to love."

"She was a great mom to our kids....and a bit of a whore. One time she gave me chlamydia. I'm still mad about it."

...no. That's just not how it's done.

We don't speak ill of the dead.

Chapter 3: Let the Games Begin

Scarlet's body moved through the pool with all the grace she had when she walked on land. She cut through the water smoothly, turning her head to pull in air. She reached the opposite side and emerged on the edge like a wet dream…her body, glistening as the water droplets formed.

"Careful, killer," Leo said as Scarlet lifted herself onto the side of the pool, "you'll give the old man a heart attack."

"You or my landlord?" Scarlet responded playfully.

"Maybe both of them," Ezra said, "but I think I can handle it."

Ezra wore plaid shorts and deck shoes. His smooth, dark skin looked good against the light purple of his cotton shirt.

"I think you can too," she said looking him up and down and biting her lip.

"Easy now, you two," Leo said.

Scarlet wrapped her towel around her waist and put her sunglasses on.

"So, what did you want to talk to us about?" Ezra asked.

......

Scarlet was working at a club in Dallas when her path crossed Old Money. She sensed it when it walked into the room. Old Money has an air about it that differs from the rest. It is arrogant and self-serving, lacks compassion and knows nothing of hard work. It takes for granted the very air encompassing it and doesn't acknowledge the sweat of the men and women that built the country it stands in.

Old Money slithers through generations creating more of the same stagnant mindset. It has soft hands and a heart made of jagged rock.

...and it was Scarlet's favorite toy.

She would be the cat and Old Money would be her mouse. She would draw him in with an invitation to play and the game would not be over until her claws were buried in his flesh.

She made eye contact.

He was captured immediately.

Beginning with her pinky, each finger following the last in a wave no one else could mimic, she called him to her.

As he approached, his heart beat a little faster and so did hers. In her eyes he could see a thousand nights of sexual fantasies. In his eyes she could see an evil that would soon concede to her rapture.

Wonder what we will have this time, she thought. *Rapist, sadist, pedophile?*

Enough liquor combined with the right questions and she had her answer.

·······

Scarlet was invited to attend a risqué event with her new friend, Old Money. He would have a dress sent over to her hotel and there would be a car to pick her up…all the extravagant things that Old Money could buy under the guise of generosity.

Scarlet knew, of course, this was a form of control but had accepted graciously and played the part of the doe-eyed stripper, with ease.

When the evening arrived, she untied the ribbon and opened the box to reveal a burgundy satin dress. The cut made it impossible for her to wear any undergarments. It fit like a custom-made glove.

When she arrived at the sprawling mansion, the driver opened the door and took her hand to help her stand. She prolonged eye contact with him a little longer than necessary and thanked him by squeezing his hand.

"Megan," she spoke seductively to the doorman. "I'm a guest of James."

He found her name on the list and stepped aside to let her pass. She walked a few steps, turned to look at him over her shoulder and gave him a wink. The tops of his ears blushed red because she had caught him checking out her ass. Scarlet didn't mind. In fact, she had counted on it.

Old Money knew her only by her stage name. He either didn't think to ask if that was her real name or he didn't really care what her name was. She was blonde and she could get him into places he couldn't get by himself.

The door opened and a sea of rich and beautiful people stretched out before her. She recognized a few famous faces and her stomach lurched as she wondered which ones were there for the secret party within the party.

Did their dates, wives and girlfriends know?

Scarlet doubted it. This was the sort of vile underground activity that wasn't even spoken of in hushed tones. This wasn't a taboo behavior like admitting to someone that you enjoy being pissed on during sex.

This was trafficking.

This was rape.

....

Scarlet could feel the rhythm of her heart beating in her throat. She felt someone would notice her veins pumping wildly underneath her pale skin, but they all seemed too infatuated with her face.

She kept her breath steady as they studied her eyes and she looked into theirs as if she knew everything about them but didn't care.

We all have monsters inside us, her eyes seemed to say. *You should let your monster out so he can play with mine. Wild and vicious lovers, they will rule with naked carnage and chaos...and then when it's over, we will put them back where they came from. Deep, deep inside the darkness of our minds, we will tuck them away...and no one will ever know.*

It wasn't that this was 'that kind of party' or that these were 'those kind of people'. That look worked on every man she had ever met. It might be interpreted differently by some. The more sentimental, the more likely they felt a deep, spiritual connection but in the end, it all came down to stirring the groin.

For many, that's where the monster lives.

Scarlet was doing her best to look casually around in between eye-fucking the guests. She was taking note of where people were entering and leaving the room. She was taking mental photography of the exits to the outside and where the guards were.

Much of her focus landed repeatedly on a staircase at the back of the room. She wondered if the large man standing at the bottom would stop her if she tried simply walking up like she belonged…

"You don't look like you belong here," a voice behind her said coolly.

Fuck, Scarlet thought. She inhaled deeply and turned slowly on her heel, making sure to use the southern drawl from her youth that she had tried so hard to leave behind.

"No? Where do I belong, then?"

He was tall and lean with a ridiculous mustache that curled up and around. His teeth were crooked and tinged with the yellow of the aging smoker. The top hat which sat upon his greasy head completed the likeness of a circus ringmaster in a low-budget porn.

He leaned in and whispered, "you should be at the REAL party, dear. The one that's going on above this one right now." He motioned, with his eyes, toward the staircase.

"Oh? This party has been so delightful. I wasn't aware there was more happening elsewhere."

His gnarled smile widened.

"You are a terrible liar, dear. The boredom is written all over your face. You don't belong here. You need more…spice. Want to come with me?" he asked as he offered his arm.

"I'd love to, but I should let my date know first. He was so kind to invite me," she continued in her sweet southern accent.

"Such a sweet girl. He won't even notice. He is…shall we say…preoccupied…at the moment."

His eyes were black and though she couldn't physically see it, Scarlet knew his soul was too. She took his arm and they began their slow ascent up the stairs and into the second realm of hell.

……….

"So how did you come to know about this upstairs party, Mister…" Scarlet trailed off even though she knew exactly who he was. She had done her research. She anticipated a face to face meeting with him would be difficult to attain, and yet, there she was arm in arm with him.

"…Sinepet, but you can call me Geoffrey, dear…and this is my home. This is my party within my party," he smiled motioning around the landing. "The downstairs is fine, but the upstairs is for the more adventurous."

"More adventurous? I love a good adventure, Geoffrey. Show me?"

97

"Yes, dear. I could tell you were one of us. There is an excitement in your eyes now that I didn't see before. I'm a great judge of character, you know."

"I bet you are."

He smiled again and pointed to a doorway. She nodded with the excitement she knew he would want to see.

As they walked slowly to the door, she braced herself for the atrocities she would see behind it. She played out the scenarios so that nothing would shock her. She planned each move carefully so that her reaction would be deliberate and calculated. She knew that reacting out of emotion would only cause messy chaos and being ready for what she saw was the only way to stay calm.

He knocked a specific knock: two short, one long, three short and then two finger taps.

The door opened...

...her mind raced...

Shit, she thought disappointedly as she took in the scene. *This isn't it. Of course, it isn't. Meeting him was the easy part. Getting him to trust me will be harder.*

It was a different kind of party than the one downstairs. There was a clown with her shirt off giving a blowjob to a man wearing a yellow tutu and a tiara, a naked old man with sagging balls was dancing on a table and some naked women were snorting coke off each other's asses. There were some sweaty men that looked like they were tripping on acid talking to a plant in the corner.

There were a lot of tits and a lot of drugs. Everyone in this room was here of their own free will, bonded together by their freakish fantasies. Any other day, this would have been a party that Scarlet enjoyed…but this isn't what she came for.

"As I suspected, you still look disappointed," Sinepet said.

He pushed her hair back from her face.

"Be patient, dear. Yes, we are going to be great friends, you and I."

……..

That night Scarlet dreamed of Vasco.

She was laughing and he was smiling at her with dimpled cheeks, pulling her by her hand playfully demanding, "come with me, love!"

She knew this memory well. This was the day she told Vasco she was pregnant. She had been horrified but he was absolutely delighted. He had picked her up and spun her around and told her that they were going to have the most beautiful baby in the world.

"Come with me, love," he had said as he pulled her through the street. "We have to get you everything you need."

She had laughed at his childlike excitement and ran her fingers through his curls when he knelt in the street to kiss her flat belly.

What a beautiful day that had been. What a beautiful dream to have to remember her Vasco.

Then, everything started to become dark and Scarlet's eyes filled with tears. Vasco's hand was no longer in hers. Something had taken him and was taking her in the opposite direction.

She was floating above the bed watching Vasco weep over her while she laid in a pool of blood.

It was the day they lost the baby.

"I don't want to see this!" she yelled into the darkness around her.

"I don't want to see him hurting! Take me back!"

There was laughter.

Deep, throaty laughter.

Her father's laughter.

Everything went black and Scarlet opened her eyes. The dream was over.

The room was dark with only a little moonlight finding its way in and spilling onto the floor like a shiny puddle. She blinked away the tears, sat up, smoothed her hair away from her face and put her hands on her belly.

Scarlet had been surprised when she found out that she was carrying Vasco's child because she had always felt that she would never have children. She had been so worried about her abilities, but Vasco's confidence made her excited for the future.

When she lost the baby during the night in her second trimester, she tried to tell herself that she knew she would never be a mother so there was nothing to be upset about. She reminded herself that she didn't want children and she would have been a terrible parent.

The truth was, she had already been a good mother to her unborn baby. She had stopped putting any chemicals into her body the moment she found out she was pregnant. So had Vasco. They made healthy choices for their diets and for their lives. Both were sober for the first time in a very long time.

The miscarriage had been devastating to both of them.

My Vasco, she thought, *my baby. Our baby.*

She rocked back and forth, alone in one of the beds in Sinepet's mansion, imagining the life she could have had again and again until Scarlet had driven herself to the brink of madness.

While there, teetering on the edge of insanity, she heard crying. It was a hopeless cry….the cry of someone who had given up.

Scarlet knew those cries and those feelings.

She knew that pain.

She took a deep breath to center herself and reminded herself why she was there. She put her feet on the floor, stood up and wound her hair into a bun on top of her head.

•••••••

The smoke rolled from Scarlet's lips like circular clouds making their way across a summer sky.

She stared out the window of her apartment in Atlanta and didn't even blink when she saw Ezra's car approaching. She didn't move from the window until she heard the knock at the door.

She breathed deep, letting it out slowly through pursed lips and opened the door. She smiled at Ezra and Leo, pretending not to notice their furrowed brows and concerned eyes.

"What a surprise!" she exclaimed throwing her arms around them. "Why didn't you call first? Come in! What brings you guys to Georgia…wait…what's wrong with you guys?"

Ezra shifted his weight from one foot to the other searching her eyes for something he seemed desperate to find.

"Ezra?" she asked with a look of confusion.

"Scarlet, I…we…" Ezra trailed off.

"We have to talk to you about the tip you gave us on the human trafficking ring in Dallas," Leo spoke in an even tone.

There was no smile on his lips nor in his eyes.

"Yeah. I saw it on the news. You guys did a great job! I'm really proud of you!" she exclaimed and smiled her million-dollar smile.

She felt Ezra's shoulders relax to her left as she looked into Leo's eyes.

"Scarlet, when you came to us with this information, we told you we couldn't go after Sinepet. There wasn't sufficient proof," Leo said. "You were noticeably angry with us. You haven't accepted our calls…"

"So, that's why you decided to take care of it? Aw…I love you guys!"

"No, Scarlet. We didn't. This wasn't us. This wasn't the government. Did you…?"

Scarlet smirked, "me? You can't be serious?"

"Well, not you. Not by yourself…but did you…organize this? It's just very strange that…"

Scarlet laughed and they both looked uncomfortable.

"You guys…seriously?" Scarlet questioned.

"It's a strange coincidence, Scar. You have to admit that," Ezra said still looking at his feet.

"So, let me get this straight. I come to you with information about a human trafficking ring that you choose not to pursue. It ends up getting busted…and as something far worse than anyone imagined, I might add….and you came all the way to Georgia to ask me if I orchestrated it? If you couldn't do it, with the FBI backing you what would possibly make you think **I** could? That's ridiculous. Get out."

"Scarlet, please, you have to understand…"

"No, Ezra, I don't. Get out."

The bathroom door opened.

A tall, lean woman stepped out and asked, "what's going on here, honey?"

"Nothing. These guys seem to think I'm responsible for breaking up that pedophile ring that just got busted in Dallas," Scarlet answered with disdain.

The raven beauty laughed and put her arm around Scarlet.

"Well, this **is** a pretty powerful bitch. Men bow down to her sexy ass from coast to coast, but Scarlet has been here with me. She hasn't been back to Dallas since she met that old sleazebag who told her about the parties."

Ezra looked relieved, but Leo looked skeptical.

"I didn't get your name," Leo said as he extended his hand to Scarlet's friend.

She closed one of her gold eyelids seductively in a wink, put her hand gently in his and pulled him a little closer.

"That's because I didn't give it to you, handsome. The name is Ryin," she said with a perfect smile.

Chapter 4: Stilettos and Stalagmites

Leo was suspicious.

He was eventually going to catch up with her. He was not blinded by the sexual adoration that Ezra felt for her. While he would have a hard time linking her to Dallas, it wasn't entirely impossible with all the new advances in DNA profiling.

Through many late-night conversations, Scarlet had learned from Ezra about DNA samples, blood spatter analysis and other innovations in criminal investigation.

She had adapted with new ways to protect herself from culpability, but she had gotten too comfortable staying in one spot. She had become a permanent fixture in her Georgia town and had cozied up in the close relationships she had built.

For the first time since the early days with Val and Vasco, she had felt like she had a family. It pained her in the pit of her stomach, but Scarlet knew it was time to go.

She left a note and three months' rent for the sweet elderly couple who owned her apartment. She phoned Ezra and told him she was going to Mexico to work for a few weeks and would call him when she returned.

She didn't call Ryin. She knew that Ezra and Leo would eventually try to track her down and she wanted Ryin to be able to say, with honesty, that she hadn't seen or spoken to her. She and Ryin were kindred spirits. Scarlet knew she would understand.

She packed her things - including a safe that contained all her money and her favorite hunting knife- Scarlet disappeared into the night.

She headed north, staying primarily along the east coast. She traded her car in for another at a small used car dealership in North Carolina. She never stayed anywhere longer than two weeks and she didn't make any friends.

She switched up her hair color three times over the course of four months. She got what she could from each club and made plenty of money to take care of herself for a while.

Scarlet had managed thus far to never be fingerprinted or x-rayed. As far as society was concerned, she didn't exist, and she wanted to keep it that way. So, when a tooth in the back of her mouth started keeping her up at night, she thought of pulling it herself but instead she stalked the clubs for a dentist that would let her in after hours.

He wasn't that hard to find.

"Thanks for seeing me like this, Doctor," she purred, tucking her short black hair behind her ear.

He chuckled and moved closer to her, breathing in her scent before pulling his mask up.

"No problem, Shaina. Let's see what's going on….yes, I see the issue. It looks like you are going to need a root canal. Let's do an x-ray and…"

"Just pull it out," she said with his hands still in her mouth.

Her stare was intense and seductive. The overhead light made the yellow ring around her pupil glow.

"Well...we need to..."

She pulled him in with her gaze and slowly shook her head no and he withdrew his hands.

"Ok," he said uncomfortably. "I'll just numb it..."

She kept his eyes locked with hers and continued, slowly shaking her head.

"It's going to hurt," he said almost frightened.

She winked, licked her lips and said, "hurt me, baby."

......

Scarlet was dreaming...

The trees poked up through the swamps - like daggers - piercing the gradient purples of the night sky. Her freedom would always look like that in her mind.

The bayou...

From her balcony, she could see the parades and feel the energy of a thousand people. The music of her city played to the tune of her soul...or was it the other way around?

New Orleans…

The city that took her in and raised her as one of its own.

The city that didn't care that she arrived underage, broke and more than a little broken. The city that opened its loving arms and turned her fragility into unbreakable solidity…while allowing her to keep the madness within…because she needed the madness to survive.

No other city could have done for Scarlet what New Orleans did.

She felt the vibrations, her hair long again, her skin still bruised from the last altercation with her father. It was the night she arrived in the city.

She saw Val.

They were kids, sharing a sandwich in an abandoned house.

Then, Vasco was waving in the distance.

It was their first real date. She remembered it like it was yesterday. She placed her hands on the side of his face…but he wasn't there.

…and she wasn't in her city.

The purple skies gave way to tan walls as her eyes fluttered open and reality settled into her soul.

She had passed out briefly.

"Aren't you going to come in here and tell me goodnight?" a man called from the shower.

Fuck, she thought. *I forgot about him.*

He was the manager of a hellhole grease pit and ran girls on the side. Scarlet overheard some dressing room talk and decided to pay him a visit. She stalked him to a grungy club and "accidentally" bumped into him.

He was even more grotesque than she had imagined. He had bragged right away and offered to make her his top girl...if he liked what she had to offer.

She assured him that she would blow his mind.

Scarlet entered the bathroom, naked, and used a towel to wipe away the condensation on the mirror. She could see his silhouette through the steamed glass in the reflection. She pushed her hair back from her eyes with her left hand and ran the fingers of the same hand across her bottom lip.

She looked tired.

She looked bored.

She was both.

She entered the shower slowly, facing him, with her back to the water. She let her right arm hang by her side and in her hand, she gripped her knife. She wasn't concerned that he would notice, and she barely tried to conceal it. He was thinking with his dick, so she knew the only way he would notice the knife is if she could somehow manage to hold it with her tits.

Oblivious, he slipped his arm around her waist to pull her in for a kiss. She allowed his mouth to linger over hers for her a moment and then she plunged the knife deeply into his abdomen. He pushed her back and searched her eyes for answers he wouldn't receive.

Her face was blank when she pulled the knife out and hit him with it a second time in the chest, this time twisting it until he tried to scream out…but she put her left hand over his mouth and held it there, slowly shaking her head back and forth, until he started to slump against her.

She pushed him away and he fell to a seated position against the shower wall opposite the faucet. She got on her knees in front of him, kissed his left cheek and pushed the knife slowly into the right side of his neck.

Scarlet stood up and let the water pour over her body, closing her eyes when it ran down her face. When she opened her eyes, she looked at the naked man bleeding out in front of her.

"Goodnight, baby," she whispered.

. . . .

Scarlet spent the night with a hot Latina woman from the club. They partied with a bottle of liquor and half a bottle of pills, went skinny dipping in her backyard pool and had steamy sex on the lanai.

"You don't get tired of moving?" she asked Scarlet, squeezing the water out of her long black hair.

"Sometimes," Scarlet answered, "but I can't slow down. I want to quit doing this shit by the time I'm forty and I want to make everything I can until then."

"Quit dancing at forty?"

"Mmm-hmm," Scarlet answered.

"You can stay in place and still dance until then," she said, motioning to her home.

It was a nice, well-kept bungalow on a quiet street outside the city. There were brightly painted accent walls throughout the home and street-inspired art on the walls. It was comfortable and inviting.

"This works...but I get too bored...and being the new girl has its perks. I stay until the newness wears off and then move to the next."

"...and to the next woman?" she asked Scarlet, moving closer.

"When I see one I like," Scarlet answered, pulling her in.

• • • • • •

Scarlet was starting to feel the effects of her stilettos. Faint lines were beginning to show on her face as decades of heavy drug use began to catch up with her.

She was also getting tired of running. She longed for the days of New Orleans or even Georgia when she had been able to plant some roots to cultivate her existence.

She missed Vasco and Val. She missed Ryin and Ezra. She missed the elderly couple and Leo.

One night after a particularly brutal night at the club, Scarlet briefly considered cutting The Puppeteers strings by ending her life.

She had set up camp in a five-star hotel in Seattle and laid out the map of her life…the map she and Vasco had dreamed over so long ago. It had become a map of death. Most of the dots covering the cities she had visited had bodies associated with them.

A lot of death.

A lot of pain.

A lot of death because **they** had caused so much pain.

They deserved death.

…but maybe she did too.

The lines start to blur when your morals are already blurry…because the goddamn Puppet Master dropped you into hell and just keeps you, dancing there.

Fuck you, Puppet King, she thought. *You won't win.*

She downed the rest of her vodka and slept in the floor.

......

If he could have recounted the story, he would have focused on how her eyes changed. She was soft and seductive…then as if a switch flipped on inside her head, she was cold and calculating. One minute, she was stroking him and then the next she was digging her nails into his skin.

She used her body to charm him…and then, she used it to hurt him.

If he could have told the police, he would have told them that there was surely a monster living inside the seductress. A vicious demon with indescribable power.

…but he would not speak to anyone again.

They found his naked body crushed against the pavement. His blood pooled around him and his leg was bent all the way back, the bone protruding through his skin.

It appeared that he had too much to drink and jumped from the balcony to his death. He was holding a note, written in his own handwriting, apologizing for what he had done to his daughter.

"Looks pretty cut and dry, boss. Looks like a suicide."

"Yeah," Leo answered squinting up toward the balcony "it does, doesn't it?"

......

Scarlet leaned back in the chair; her red satin robe was open and draped around her shoulders. She ran her fingers through her hair, closed her eyes and tilted her head back. The voluptuous blonde on her knees in front of her, with her face buried between Scarlet's legs was the first woman Scarlet met when she arrived in Northern California.

Though Scarlet generally preferred one-night stands and no names, the two women had spent the last three days together in Scarlet's hotel room on the west shore of Lake Tahoe. From the windows and balcony, they could see the tall trees on the south shore and the snow-capped mountain peaks in the distance. The deep blue water was as smooth as glass and the air smelled clean and refreshing.

She was enjoying the rest and relaxation...almost as much as she was enjoying her sexy blonde snow bunny...but Scarlet knew it was time to move south and find a new club.

Time to head back to the night...to the stage and the lights that always welcomed her in like an old friend. The clubs never cared how fucked up she was. They didn't care that she was a little dark underneath it all.

The clubs preferred her that way, actually.

They accepted her however she came...as long as she came in hot.

...and Scarlet always came in hot.

Chapter 5: The Dollhouse

The 90's brought more attention to strip clubs as some dancers worked the poles all the way to Hollywood. It wasn't as easy to hide inside the walls as it had been. It wasn't as easy to hide anywhere.

Cameras were becoming common even at the worst establishments and a life of anonymity was becoming nearly impossible to achieve.

Scarlet decided to burn her map and ditch her knife.

She had been a little sad to watch the map burn. It was after all, the only story of her life there was to tell. It wasn't a story anyone needed to know...but it was still a shame to watch it lost to the flames. It had been a map of silent victory - of sorts; victory for all those who had suffered at the hands of her victims.

Were the men Scarlet killed "victims"? By society's standards, yes. By Scarlet's? No. They were abusers and they were brought to justice. In a world that never would have given them what they deserved; Scarlet ended their reign of terror.

Getting rid of her knife was just as difficult for Scarlet. It was like saying goodbye to an old friend...but it would have tied her to at least two dozen murders on the east coast alone.

Scarlet had to adapt in order to move forward.

She was tired of the game but too deep in not to win it. She was getting tired of the clubs and the drugs, but she was also getting tired of constantly moving around.

She had been working at a club aptly named The Dollhouse for two months and was considering putting down some roots like she had in Atlanta.

The club was an upscale gentlemen's paradise in southern California. The outside looked like a casino and the inside looked like a lodge. There were 6 stages and 14 private rooms, though Scarlet did her best to avoid the rooms.

No matter how much she reiterated that there was no touching – even behind closed doors – or that no amount of money would get them into her panties, they always seemed to think the rules didn't apply to them once the door to the room was closed.

So, Scarlet found it easier, and still very lucrative, to only do tableside dances at $25 per song. The DJ usually cut the songs at three minutes…and the guys usually got at least four songs in a row at a time.

The shifts were six hours so Scarlet would usually leave with at least $800 after tip-out and that was often with paying the DJ to skip her stage sets.

She was two shots into the evening when she approached a well-built man standing in front of a sign at the entrance.

The sign read:

DON'T TOUCH THE DOLLS!

"What happens if I touch them?" he asked Scarlet before turning to look at her.

"Some of us bite, some of us cry and some of us crumble…like the old porcelain dolls in the back of your grandmother's closet. Best not break the dolls…or they might break you," Scarlet answered coolly.

He turned at that statement…and he instantly adored her. He thought she was fascinating, charming and gorgeous. She was everything he wanted. He took her hand and held her at arm's length, spinning her slowly in a circle to get a good look at every part of her.

"You really are the perfect doll. I **need** you," he said with a desperation in his voice that Scarlet understood immediately.

There was kindness in his eyes…and respect. Unlike most of the patrons, his 'need' didn't have anything to do with his dick. His 'need' was for companionship.

"I'm all yours," she replied as they looked knowingly into one another's eyes.

They smiled at each other, two exquisite people who had finally found exactly what they were looking for.

They were married, in Vegas, two months later.

……

Scarlet looked good in an evening gown. She could feign interest in the most boring conversation and her smile could bring men to their knees. She was intelligent, witty and everyone loved her.

Scarlet was the perfect wife.

William Henderson was the owner of a multi-million-dollar construction company in Colorado. He was handsome and kind. He showered her with compliments and gifts.

William was the perfect husband.

Scarlet and William both felt complete for the first time in a long time. They held each other close as they danced at a charity gala on Christmas Eve.

Her sleek green satin gown was backless, and her long ponytail swung with her hips as she moved.

"I will never be able to thank you enough for coming into my life," William said sincerely to his bride as he gently moved her across the dance floor.

"You saved me too, baby," she smiled up at him.

"Are you ready to get out of here?" he asked.

"You know me, I've been ready to leave since we got here," she laughed.

They felt the eyes of the world on them as they left the ballroom, hand in hand.

They sat close to one another in the back of the limo, talking and laughing all the way to the three-story mansion that they called home. William held Scarlet's hand in his to help her as she got out of the car.

Scarlet paused in the lavish entry to wait for William.

Beneath the chandelier, two sprawling staircases faced one another. Scarlet would ascend the left staircase and walk through the large French doors to her beautiful master suite. There would be a sweet-smelling bath drawn for her and she would revel in her happiness as she watched the candlelight dance off the glass panels in her high-end custom bathroom.

William would ascend the staircase to the right and walk through the large French doors to his master suite, as well, but instead of a bath, he would revel in his happiness with the love of his life, Levi, who would be waiting for him.

"Sleep well, darling," William said, kissing Scarlet on the forehead.

"See you guys in the morning, honey," Scarlet returned wrapping her arms around his waist.

. . . .

The world they lived in at the time wasn't ready for William and Levi.

It was much more comfortable with William and Scarlet.

Outside the home, Scarlet and William were the face of a company, a community and a lifestyle that other couples longed to emulate. Scarlet was always classy, with beautiful chestnut curls that fell just beneath her shoulders. Her perfectly manicured hands moved around her fluidly as she spoke. William was in his early fifties, tall with muscles that rippled beneath his form fitting dress shirts. He shaved his head completely bald and carried himself with an air of confidence.

Inside their home…their hide-a-way…their safehouse…the power couple was William and Levi.

Levi Moody was shorter than William, though still much taller than Scarlet. His features were darker than William's. He had a slim build, a groomed beard and dimples. He had a wall full of degrees but made his money from the medical supply company he owned and operated.

William and Levi had been together for 7 years before Scarlet and William met at The Dollhouse. The love that the two men had was deep and lasting. It reminded Scarlet of her and Vasco. Sometimes it made her heart soar and other times it brought sadness. Sadness because of the love she had lost and sadness because her friends couldn't celebrate their love in public spaces.

For the most part, their lives were perfect.

…but when Levi would sit with Scarlet while she was getting ready for an event, she could see the underlying sadness in his eyes. She could feel his pain of being left behind.

"I still think you should come with us," Scarlet said as she dabbed more gloss on her lips.

She had traded in her signature red for a nude color many years prior…around the same time she gave up her cigarettes.

"Maybe one day," he said.

"Times are changing, Levi. It is safer now."

"It is safer than it was…but people are still vicious, sweetie. It could ruin Bill's company and he's worked so hard to build it into…"

"I know, sugar. I know. I love you," Scarlet said.

"Love you more," Levi replied genuinely.

"…and I love you both," William said from the doorway. He crossed the room and put his arm around Levi. "You know I wish things were different, my love. One day…"

"I know, Bill. I know. I love you and I promise, I understand."

Scarlet stood and after taking in her appearance, both men clapped.

"Stop it, you two…just kidding…never stop!" she smiled and pretended to curtsey.

"Most beautiful doll in The Dollhouse," William said.

•••••••

Before they were married, Scarlet told William that she was on the run from her past and he helped her escape it willingly. He and Levi accepted her as she was, broken pieces and all. They provided everything she could ever need or want except for sex…and that was never an issue for Scarlet.

She rather enjoyed sex with herself…and in the event she needed more, she was free to find it.

She finally had a real family again.

…and money looked good on Scarlet.

She wore only the best. William and Levi would not have it any other way. She had always had an affinity for shoes, and they loved to spoil her.

Wrapped in silk robes, they would enjoy long nights by the outdoor fire, sipping wine and telling stories of their youth. Though Scarlet could never tell them everything, she still shared pieces of her life that she had never shared with anyone. They laughed together, cried together and they took care of one another.

Her years with the boys in Colorado were some of the best of her life.

The 7,200 square-foot stone mansion was a sight to behold on the Colorado skyline. William had designed it and overseen the construction himself, insisting that every detail be perfect. He had built it for he and Levi…but Scarlet fit in so well, it often seemed that they always knew she was coming.

Inside, vaulted ceilings and oak floors made the large rooms feel even larger. There were six bedrooms, two living spaces with fireplaces, a gourmet kitchen with a massive island, a bar and a room with a large screen they used to watch movies.

The back of the house had a total of thirty-six windows between the three floors and no matter which window you looked out, the view was stunning. The outside was as beautiful and well-planned as the inside. Stone paths led to a rock waterfall and sparkling luxury pool.

The pool was Scarlet's favorite part. The weather in Colorado only allowed for limited use but during those months, Scarlet lived in and by the pool. She would stretch out on a float and watch the reflection of the sun dancing off the three stories of floor to ceiling windows on the back of the house.

There was a covered deck, an outdoor kitchen and down another stone path, a gazebo. They could see the snow-capped mountains in the distance and watch the leaves change in the fall.

Scarlet often felt like she had finally outrun her fate.

Perhaps the Puppet King had forgotten about her.

…or maybe he was just allowing her a false sense of security so what was to come would be that much worse.

Chapter 6: To Have and to Hold

"...so, there he was, looking so handsome..." Levi was smiling at William while he spoke.

"...and there he was, looking like the love of my life..." William smiled back.

Scarlet was stretched out in a lounger by the pool with her wine glass. Beneath her sheer black swim robe, her red bikini had sparkling stone embellishments around the top. She wore a large sun hat to protect her pale skin from the sun. Her sunglasses shielded her eyes from the rays but also hid the tears forming in her eyes.

She loved hearing the stories of how the boys met and of their first years together.

There was nothing as pure as the love they had for one another. They both said they had known instantly that they were looking at their future. They both said time stopped.

Scarlet knew that feeling. It had happened only once - the night she met Vasco - and would never happen again...but at least it was an experience she was able to have.

An individual's feelings and experiences help them understand the feelings and experiences of others. Scarlet's life hadn't been much like anyone else's, so she was thankful for the times she felt like she was part of the rest of the world.

She was so grateful that, even if it was fleeting, she had the time with Vasco so she could understand how beautiful and deep the love was between William and Levi.

That kind of love is worth fighting for.

......

She was home alone and decided it was time for a little self-love.

Scarlet found her favorite dildo in her nightstand and pulled her shirt over her head. She pushed her panties to the side, already wet and pressed the vibrator against the outside of her body. She closed her legs together and rode it until the wave came and she saw stars in her head.

She was ready for round two when the doorbell startled her. She wasn't expecting anyone, and she had a bad feeling in her gut. She jumped up, cock in hand like a sword at the ready.

What the fuck, she thought, looking at the dildo in her hand. *What will you do with that, Scarlet? Run at them threatening to fuck them?*

She paused and raised her eyebrows.

*Hmmm. That's actually not a bad idea. Imagine the fear in the hearts of men if you came running at them – electric dick in hand screaming "I **will** FUCK you..."*

She took it to the bathroom, put it in the sink to deal with later and started out the bedroom door.

Huge windows surrounded the heavy wooden double doors. She could see out, but her uninvited guest couldn't see in. Looking out of the windows to the circular drive, there was no mistaking that the car outside was an unmarked government issue.

Shit, she thought. *He found me.*

She didn't have to see his face to know.

It was Leo.

As it had so many times before, Scarlet's life changed in an instant. Standing on the staircase, tits still out, Scarlet knew this was the beginning of the end.

......

When William arrived home that evening, Levi and Scarlet were holding one another on the sofa. Scarlet's luggage was packed. Levi looked up with tears in his eyes and William knew immediately.

"No," William protested.

"He found me," Scarlet said. "It's time, William. I have to go."

"Is there no other way? I can hire the best attorney for you, honey. We can get you out of this," William's voice broke as the tears came.

"No amount of money can get me out of this, baby. You have done more than enough for me. You loved me. You kept me safe. You gave me a family and a home....but you can't protect me from what's coming. No one can," Scarlet continued to speak as she stood, "but I can protect you and Levi by leaving."

"Will we see you again, darling?" Levi asked.

Scarlet just shook her head and fought back tears of her own.

......

William opened the door to a man in a black suit. He had a strong jawline and medium brown hair that was beginning to gray at the temples. He made his introduction; flashed his badge.

It was Leo.

Leo told William he needed to speak with his wife, so William invited him into the den. After offering his guest a beverage, he crossed the room to an ornate wooden table in the entry with a large matching mirror hanging on the wall above it.

He opened the drawer, retrieved a handwritten note and gave it to the agent.

Dearest William,

By the time you read this, I'll be on my way to Argentina. Please don't waste your resources trying to find me.

I never wanted to hurt you, but I met someone, and we need a fresh start.

I just couldn't bear to see the disappointment on your face.

Always,
Camelia

"I called our travel agent and they confirmed, Camelia booked a ticket to Argentina the day before she left this note. She's gone."

"Did your wife ever talk about her past?" Leo asked.

William shook his head.

"I have reason to believe her name isn't Camelia. It's Scarlet…and I've been looking for her for quite some time."

......

After Leo left, William poured a drink and sat down outside. Levi joined him and they both stared at the pool for a long time as if they could still see her there.

"You think she'll be ok?" Levi asked.

William put his arm around Levi and Levi sunk in, leaning his head onto William's shoulder.

"She is tough. Tougher than you know…or even what I know," he answered. "She will be ok."

"What about us? What do we do without our girl?" Levi asked.

"We will miss her…probably forever…but we move forward. It's what she wanted us to do…and it's what I want. I want you to marry me Levi. I want us to go public."

Levi smiled through his tears.

"What if the world isn't ready?" he asked.

"Fuck the world. I'm ready. You're ready."

Levi sat up straight and leaned forward in his seat.

"What about the business, Bill?"

"Remember that offer I got awhile back? That man in San Antonio that wanted to buy the business? I've been thinking about it. I'm going to sell it to him."

Levi's took his glasses off and turned toward William.

"Really? Are we really doing this, Bill?"

William took his hand.

"That depends, my love. Are you saying 'yes'?"

"Yes!" Levi answered, laughing through the tears, "Yes! Of course, the answer is yes!"

......

BOOK THREE

"LOOK AT ME!

I'm pissed off, Armani. You are being so **fucking** rude right now. Look at me when I'm talking. Have you been listening to what I've been trying to tell you? I was trapped. No matter where I went...no matter what I did. I was trapped in this fucking shitshow with someone else pulling the strings, right? He took everything from me at every turn...this Puppet King...this bastard writing out the scenes of my life for his own twisted pleasure.

STAY WITH ME!

Are you **really** trying to die right now? You don't get to die until I kill you...and I'm not going to kill you until I'm done telling you the story of my (her) life. That's how this works. You and I are both running out of time, Armani...but it isn't time yet. You will die when **I** say you will die.

OPEN YOUR EYES!

Come on... Armani, I shared my drugs with you. You didn't deserve that courtesy. Keep your fucking eyes open until I tell you to close them. I need someone to see me one last time. Someone to hear me before it's all over and I cut these strings. I won't let you or this sick puppeteer win. Not today. Not ever.

WE **BOTH** DESREVE THIS!

Oh...don't get me wrong...we both deserve the death that's coming for us. You are a disgusting mother fucker, Armani...the worst kind of garbage human...a rapist and an abuser. You deserve to die and

I'm going to kill you in the worst way…because I deserve to be the one to do it. I deserve the pleasure of watching you suffer until the end.

…but ultimately, I deserve to die too, don't I?

Chapter 1: Into the Wild

Scarlet paced the floor of her hotel room like a caged tiger hungry for the hunt…and looking for an escape to wreak carnage on the world that imprisoned her.

The walls were closing in and she needed a plan. Leo would never stop looking for her. She couldn't – wouldn't – kill Leo. She had never killed a man that didn't deserve to die…and Leo was a good man.

He's just doing his job, she thought. *Protecting and serving the people…but isn't that what I've been doing too?*

She knew she never should have told Leo about the human trafficking ring in Dallas. She never should have trusted anyone else to handle something…no… **someone** like Sinepet. He had hidden behind his money for decades…and the government allowed it.

Leo never would have suspected her if she had just taken care of it from the beginning instead of asking for help. She knew better. She knew better than to believe there was anyone out there who could handle the situation – especially a man - who could have handled **any** of the situations she had handled.

What Sinepet needed was exactly what he got: a slow, painful death at the hands of the all-in-one judge, jury and executioner. Of all the men who died by Scarlet's hand, she replayed the killing of Geoffrey Sinepet the most in her mind.

No one deserved to die more than him.

Sinepet had invited her to stay in one of his guest rooms the night of the party. Scarlet had closed her eyes to let some of the drugs wear off so she could function and woke to the sound of a young girl crying. She followed the sound to a bookcase with a large man guarding it.

She used a weapon of opportunity, a vase nearby, and smashed it over his head from behind. He hadn't been paying attention because he wasn't there to guard anything. He was more of a lookout if there was a police raid...and there would never be a police raid.

She briefly considered killing him – the man who stood outside and listened to the cries of pain, but she decided to focus on whatever was behind the faux door.

She looked for and found a lever. As she suspected, the bookcase was indeed a door. Behind the door, a hallway with 6 doors on either side and one large one at the end of the hall.

She opened the first door on her left, slowly, not wanting to make the slightest sound, and clenched her teeth in anger at what she saw. A young girl - no more than 13 - was being raped by an obese man with a bad toupee. Scarlet crept up, quietly, and picked his belt up from the floor. She was on his back and strangling him with it before he knew what happened.

She pushed his lifeless, worthless body off the girl and whispered in her ear, "get dressed, go downstairs and hide. I will come for you when I'm done."

...and Scarlet repeated the process...going through each door...becoming angrier and angrier...killing each man she found more violently than the last...telling each girl the same thing..."go find the others...I will come for you"...

She particularly enjoyed killing the man who had brought her to the party as his guest. Old Money was in the seventh room she entered. After freeing his victim, she dragged him to a mirror and made him watch while she slit his throat from one side to the other.

As she had suspected, the last door was the worst…and made her the angriest. She didn't attempt silence this time. She burst in, covered in the blood of Sinepet's special guests – his paying guests - and made herself known.

Her eyes were wild, and her jaw was set.

Sinepet stood, his pale, lanky body frozen with fear. His greasy hair hung in his face. He called out confidently…but no one came.

"They can't hear you, Geoffrey. Everybody's dead. I killed them. I killed them all," Scarlet laughed maniacally. "I saved you for last and I'm going to hurt you the worst."

Sinepet reached for a weapon but Scarlet was already too close. She grabbed him by his limp dick with her left hand and twisted until he screamed. He used both hands to try to remove her grip. Using he right hand, she picked up one of the devices he had been using to torture his underage victim and bashed him in the head with it. His blood spattered all over her face and she spit it back onto him.

Sinepet fell to his knees in front of her, swaying in and out of consciousness…she motioned to the child on the bed to get out…but realized the child wasn't moving. She left Sinepet and checked on the girl.

Her small body was covered in cuts and bruises…and she was dead.

Scarlet gritted her teeth, ran at Sinepet and slapped him hard across his face. His head fell back and to the right. But she grabbed his hair and jerked his head back, so he was looking into her eyes.

"There is no way to kill you that is violent enough to satisfy me," Scarlet said, "but I'm going to try so hard, vile waste of humanity. I'm going to make sure you hurt more than you ever have…and that it takes a really, really long time for you to die, you filthy fucking bastard …because you deserve that. You deserve to die in the worst possible way."

Sinepet tried to stand but Scarlet sliced his chest with a knife from his own collection and stuck her fingers into the wound.

Sinepet screamed.

Scarlet laughed.

"That's it…cry for me, baby. I want you to cry. I want you to scream. I want you to long for salvation that will never come…and I want you to know…if this isn't hell…then when I get there, I will find you again and we will do this for eternity."

......

"In 1993, the cops got a call from the Sinepet mansion and arrived to find 12 traumatized and victimized underage girls in the living room. There were 12 more in the basement and one deceased child's body found in a room in a hidden hallway on the top floor.

The bodies of 13 men, including Sinepet, were also found in the hidden space. Some with their cocks chopped clean off. Sinepet had been tortured the most and appeared to have suffered the longest. They never recovered his missing genitals.

Three large men who worked for Sinepet as bodyguards were found alive - but bound and gagged at their posts…and no one claims to have seen anything…or anyone," he looked up from the file he was reading from and continued with a furrowed brow, "and you think this one girl did it…by herself?"

"Woman…not girl…and I know it sounds crazy, boss, but she came to us only a week before these murders and asked us to look into it. The timeline fits…and I like her for a lot of other brutal murders across the country."

"Across the country? So, one girl – sorry…**woman**… has gone on a brutal cross-country serial-killing spree without ever being detected…without anyone ever coming forward? Look, Leo, you're a good detective. One of the best, but this seems…pretty far-fetched."

He adjusted his thick glasses, pushing them farther into his bushy eyebrows.

"She moves around, goes by different names and changes her appearance…" Leo started before being interrupted.

"…and co-workers, friends, family? They don't find it odd that she's always changing…and moving…and killing?"

"She works in the clubs as a dancer…"

"A titty dancer, Leo? You think a TITTY DANCER…"

"Sir, with all due respect, I don't think you should call them…"

"Leo, go home. Get some rest."

136

"Sir…"

"That's an order, Leo."

. . . .

Leo walked through his apartment door, placed his jacket on the sofa and ran his hands through his hair. He tugged at the knot in his tie, exhaled deeply and unbuttoned the first 2 buttons of his shirt.

I'm going to have to bring her in myself, he thought. *On my own, without the bureau.*

He knew it was her. Everyone thought he was crazy…but he knew in his bones that it was her.

He had known since she disappeared from Atlanta – without a trace – after he had confronted her about Sinepet in Dallas…and it had consumed his life since then.

Six years.

For six years, he researched every unsolved case involving men connected to strip clubs and pored over the Sinepet case. His obsession with Scarlet had affected his job, his marriage and his life. It was all he could think about.

…and now that his marriage had ended, it was all he had left.

He sat down at his desk, piled high with manilla folders, and looked at his "Scarlet Wall"…a giant map of the United States with every murder he thought she had committed marked with a sticker and a date.

It all adds up, darlin'...and I know it's you, he thought. *Where did you go this time?*

He searched the map with his eyes narrowed.

I know you didn't go to Argentina...and I know you left that note with William Henderson for me.

Leo stood up and paced the room.

...like a caged tiger...hungry for the hunt...

......

Though she and Levi would occasionally have two of his anti-anxiety pills with their wine on a Friday night, Scarlet hadn't done any illicit drugs since she left The Dollhouse.

In her hotel room, alone and bored, she found herself wanting more than what was waiting at the bottom of her Gin and Dubonnet.

Downstairs, in the lobby, Scarlet asked the attendant where people in the area went to dance.

The music could change, and the drugs of choice could change but one thing that never changed was the relationship between dance and drugs.

The primal feeling of pushing emotion outward through the body to the sound of the bass pumping underneath the melody...bodies moving together in the dark...with the lights pulsating overhead...

Add the void filling, heightened sensation that the drugs brought to the table and the pleasure seekers in the brain send bursts and waves of pure excitement through the body with every beat...

It was a helluva combo...and had been for decades.

Scarlet's short burgundy sweater dress showed off her best assets and her matching suede boots hit her at just the right spot on her smooth thighs. She pulled her hat down over her ears and adjusted her scarf before entering the winter breeze.

It was a nice night in Downtown Houston in January of 2001, but Scarlet was searching for something with a little more bite and a lot more bass.

......

The first person she talked to tried to buy her a drink. He was close to forty with bleach- blonde hair and he introduced himself to her by his DJ name.

Scarlet laughed at him and he scurried away.

She bought herself a few drinks and eventually found what she was looking for.

She didn't care for EDM, so she didn't intend to stay.

…but then the little mouse caught her eye.

The DJ was walking a young woman out the back door. The woman was slumped over and leaning heavily on him.

It didn't look - nor did it feel - right to Scarlet.

She finished her drink, laid some money on the bar and followed them out the door.

The alley was dark, but she could see silhouettes near some large garbage cans. One was moving but the other was completely still.

Scarlet reached around the hat and scarf she had pushed into the bottom of her purse and found her black leather gloves, slipping them on her hands as she approached the shadows.

"What's going on over there?" she asked.

"Hey, it's just me, DJ…" he began to explain but Scarlet cut him off.

"I don't give a fuck about you…nor do I care about your occupation. I was speaking to the lady," Scarlet spat at him more angrily than she intended.

She looked around the cans and saw what she expected to see. The woman was out cold. Her shirt and skirt were lifted. The man was trying to stuff his rather small penis back into his pants.

"Well, look at you," Scarlet said, narrowing her eyes. "DJ Lameass can't find a woman that wants him…so he has to drug one?"

"No…it's not what it looks like. She was totally into it," he stammered.

"Into it?" Scarlet laughed maniacally. "She is **unconscious**," she continued stepping closer.

"Listen, I don't want any trouble here…"

"Trouble? DJ Fuckface, you ARE the trouble. You and all the men like you…FUCK. I just wanted some drugs. I just wanted one fucking night of drugs and happiness…and LOOK!"

Scarlet pulled a knife from her purse and set her purse down on the ground.

"Wh---", he started.

"NOW, you've ruined my night and my bag, DJ Dumbnuts," she said, pointing the knife at her purse. " But more importantly, you've ruined that woman's life. You have no idea how she will feel FOREVER knowing she was violated."

Scarlet was walking slowly toward him.

"I didn't do anything!" he pleaded as he stepped backward.

"Maybe not tonight…because I interrupted but you were going to…and this wasn't your first time, DJ Twatass."

"M-m-my name is Justin and I promise I will never do it again if you just let me go!"

"Oh? Justin, huh? **Now** you don't want to be a DJ? That's ok, Justin, it doesn't really matter who or what you want to be."

He turned to run but tripped over his own feet and fell on his stomach.

Scarlet jumped onto his back, lifted his head by his bleached straw hair and slit his throat. He tried to grab at his neck, but she pressed her knees deep into his back.

She stayed until it was over.

Then, she stood, wiped her knife off on the back of his jacket, dusted herself off and headed back to the woman by the garbage cans.

Scarlet wrapped the knife with her scarf and pushed it deep into her bag along with her gloves.

To have her here like this, like garbage, Scarlet thought. *Poor baby.*

She was able to spare this one…but how many more? How many more were out there?

She fixed the young woman's clothes and helped her to her feet. She was able to open her eyes and walk with Scarlet's help. They walked out of the alley and down the busy street until Scarlet found a diner.

Scarlet waited with her until she was sober enough to call someone she trusted.

"I can't thank you enough for helping me tonight," she said.

Scarlet hugged her and said, "it was no problem, honey. We have to watch out for one another. We may not be in this together, but none of us are in it alone."

......

Scarlet returned to her hotel, showered and packed her bags. She had planned on staying for at least a week, but there wasn't any time to look for cameras in the alley and she knew there were some inside the club.

She had been wearing a wig and she used an alias, but she wasn't going to take any chances. She wasn't going to be brought down by a wannabe DJ with a small dick and no game.

Scarlet drove east out of Texas and threw the wig away at a gas station in Louisiana. She threw the knife out of the passenger window and into the bayou below the bridge without even slowing down.

Seeing the exit sign for New Orleans tugged at her heart but she didn't stop driving until she hit the Florida line.

......

She was wearing a tight black dress with white stripes down the sides, tall white heels, a brown wig and brown contact lenses.

The quality of wigs had improved exponentially over the years and Scarlet preferred them to constantly cutting and dying her own hair. If a situation went south, she could throw a wig in the trash, take out her lenses and walk right out the same door she came in.

"So why don't you eat meat?" he asked with his mouth full.

He was a grotesque man...and not just in his barbarian eating habits. He had a large nose, the blood vessels broken from years of severe alcohol abuse. His bottom teeth were crooked, and the gum line was covered in thick, yellow plaque.

Scarlet read a story about him in the newspaper. He raped his assistant and he was a suspect in his first wife's murder.

He had never been held accountable for his actions.

He was slurping and smacking his food. Scarlet tried not to make a disgusted face...and had to try even harder to refrain from diving across the table to stab him in the throat.

"Animals are innocent souls. They don't deserve to die for my sustenance when I have the luxury of so many other options," Scarlet explained.

She leaned forward so he could see more of her inviting cleavage. She knew it was a pointless explanation. The people who asked that question never really wanted to know why she didn't eat meat...they just wanted to tell her why she should.

"Man's eyes are forward on their face. That means they are meat-eaters and hunters," he said.

"I didn't say I wasn't a hunter," Scarlet responded, winking and taking a long sip from her glass of chardonnay.

"So, what do you hunt, then?" he asked.

"I prefer a certain type of Big Game. Not at all innocent and remarkably arrogant," she answered, smiling.

••••••

Chapter 2: Time Will Tell

The writer of her life script was at it again and time was catching up with her.

Fucking sadist, she thought. *Fucking piece of shit sadist-puppet-master-fucker.*

Scarlet held her hair up, looking into the mirror at her naked body. She turned to the side, letting her hair fall to the middle of her back and smoothed her hands over her hips. She turned her back to the mirror and looked over her shoulder at her reflection.

Not terrible, she thought, *but you are not what you once were, princess.*

She crossed the room to the bag on her bed and unzipped it. It was full of stacks of cash William and Levi had given her before she had left them. It was enough to hold her over for several years if she handled it correctly, but she would have to scale back the lifestyle she had become accustomed to.

She had left the fake note for William to hand off to Leo...because Leo would know it was meant for him.

"...don't waste your resources trying to find me..."

Leo would know that Argentina was a ploy...but just in case, William paid a young woman and gave her all his wife's documents. They sent the new Camelia to Argentina on a very long vacation...or a chance to start a new life for herself, if she preferred.

The new Camelia's only job was to wait three months and then mail the signed divorce papers she had been given back to William so he could file them.

Camelia's fake documents had been acquired for Scarlet by William, in the first place. After they met at The Dollhouse, Scarlet told William what she could about her life, and he made the arrangements for her new identity, Camelia Bennett, before they were married.

After their nuptials in Vegas, she became Camelia Henderson.

They had both gone to great lengths to avoid being photographed together at the galas they attended and all articles about William and his business only featured photos of William, per his request.

…but they hadn't been careful enough.

Since their photograph showed up in a prominent newspaper, William, Scarlet and Levi had been preparing for the day she would have to flee.

They had prepared financially but there was no way to truly prepare emotionally. Scarlet missed her boys beyond words…and back home, she knew the boys missed her too…but Scarlet had no choice but to compartmentalize those feelings for now.

She reluctantly tucked them into the place where she kept her feelings about Vasco, Val, Ryin…and the tiniest of memories she could still conjure up about her mother.

Every good thing was gone again. She felt empty and alone…but more than that, she was reminded that she was damned from the beginning…and would be until the end.

She laid back onto the hotel bed and stared at the ceiling.

Fucking Puppet King.

"Fuck you," Scarlet said aloud. "Fuck your mother…if you have one. Fuck these strings that have turned into chains. If I could, I would wrap these chains around your neck instead of mine."

Fuck the Puppet Master and this entire excuse for a fucking show, she thought. *If this isn't hell then when I die, I will find him and burn him alive.*

She was startled by the sound of her own delirious laughter.

......

She popped two of the pills she'd gotten at the shitty EDM club in Houston and chased them down with the frozen daquiri she bought at her beachside hotel in West Palm.

She sat down and dug her toes into the cool sand, closed her eyes and listened to the waves rolling through the water and breaking onto the shore. She could see the yellow of the tiki torches even with her eyes closed.

The evening was the only time Scarlet liked the beach. It wasn't too hot, and she didn't have to worry about burning her tits off in the blazing sun.

It was calming, the waves and the stillness.

"Hey, there, sexy," a man's voice said over her.

Fucking FUCK. Goddamn motherfucking fucker. Why do men think they can fucking talk to me any fucking time they want?

Scarlet opened her eyes to a crotch in her face. A man was standing over her with his hand out like he wanted her to take it.

She smacked his hand away.

"Hey there, balls-in-my-face, how about you move the fuck along?" Scarlet asked rhetorically.

The stranger laughed and moved out of the way.

"Damn, sorry, I was just trying to help you up."

Scarlet raised her eyebrows and answered, "do I look like I fell down?"

He put his hands up like he was surrendering.

"Ok. Ok. I thought you might want some company. You don't have to be a bitch."

Scarlet stood up with the intention of beating him to death with her bare hands. She clenched her fist but regained her composure.

She relaxed her body and remembered who she was.

"I need you to learn something today. When a woman is sitting by herself you should **never** assume that she wants company. **Never** walk up to a woman when her eyes are closed and **never**, EVER, put your dick in her face unless she specifically asks for your specific dick in her specific face."

"Damn…damn…ok…don't get crazy…"

"No…this is calm. Crazy is what I'm going to do to you if you don't save yourself by leaving right now. You have three seconds to move down the beach and the hell away from me or I'm going to show you a brand new meaning of 'fire crotch'," she said calmly, placing her hand on the staff of the nearest tiki torch.

He shook his head, turned on his heel and walked away.

Scarlet inhaled slowly and exhaled slowly.

She sat back down, dug her toes into the sand, closed her eyes and waited on the buzz to kick in.

……

The next morning, Scarlet felt like shit.

She held her warm coffee cup to her forehead and rolled it back and forth. She splashed water on her face. She took a shower. Nothing helped.

Fuck, she thought. *Now I can't even handle a few pills? What the fuck is this elderly bullshit?*

She stepped out onto the balcony. The view was breathtaking, but it was too hot and too bright. She sat down in the chair anyway. Behind her sunglasses, she closed her eyes and listened to the waves.

You're getting old, bitch, she thought. *You still look good…but how much longer will that last? You can't dance. You can't get high. What are you going to do to pass the time now?*

She opened her eyes and saw a couple in the water below. He was behind her and when the waves were low, Scarlet could see he had his arm around her waist.

I guess I could seek out some human interaction…but even that sounds boring.

It was early and there weren't a lot of people out and about yet but the orange bikini in the water caught her eye. Scarlet leaned onto the balcony's edge and squinted into the distance.

Great. My old ass needs glasses now, too?

The couple was emerging from the water and Scarlet saw that it wasn't a couple, at all. It was a man and a young teenage girl. The girl had her arms crossed and looked disgusted…ashamed.

Scarlet wanted to scream from the balcony that it wasn't her fault. She wanted to leap from the ledge and kill him on the spot.

Who is that, I wonder? Your dad or your step-dad? Uncle or your Mom's new friend?

She would find out soon enough…and he would be dead by morning.

Suddenly, Scarlet felt like she would enjoy a little human interaction, after all.

• • • • • •

Fucking pedophiles are the worst, Scarlet thought, washing the blood off her hands in the cool ocean foam that covered the shore.

She picked up some wet sand, rubbed it into her hands and underneath her nails. Then, she rinsed her hands again and continued her evening stroll down the beach.

It was such a splendid evening to enjoy a walk along the shoreline.

Maybe I'd like to settle down on a beach somewhere, she thought. *I could get used to nights like this.*

The sky was clear; a million stars twinkled in and out of the black sky above her. The sand was wet and hard along the water's edge, turning soft and silky beneath her bare feet when the surf came in.

The air was a little warmer than it had been the previous evenings but still much cooler than the day.

She inhaled deeply and the salty air filled her lungs.

Exhale.

Inhale.

Exhale.

Maybe a beach in France? Scarlet asked herself. *I've always wanted to go to France.*

She had picked up a little French living in New Orleans and sometimes used it in the clubs.

Le monde est à moi.

(The world is mine.)

Scarlet smiled.

Ahead, the welcoming lights of her hotel were shining brightly in the distance. Behind her, a body in the darkness…and between them, Scarlet's footprints were disappearing almost as quickly as she made them.

• • • • • •

Scarlet reluctantly left the beach and headed north. She stopped off in a few major cities, took in some tourist sites and read every book she could get her hands on.

She swam, she ate, she had dreams of her life before… or sometimes, of a different life altogether…but she always woke up in a hotel room, alone.

She would find a little mouse to stalk and that would appease her but only until he met his demise. Then, the boredom would kick in all over again.

Finding something to do when that happened was exhausting.

She was sitting on a blanket, under a tree when a dog came running up to her and jumped in her lap, excitedly licking her face.

"Oh, my goodness…you are adorable…" Scarlet said in the child-like voice humans reserve for speaking to babies and small animals.

She put down the book she had been reading and gave the puppy some ear scratches and a belly-rub. She didn't see anyone in the park that seemed to be looking for a dog, so she went back to giving him all of her attention.

"What's your name?" she asked.

"His name is Jazz," a man's voice said behind her.

Scarlet turned toward the voice, still holding the small dog in front of her face.

"Well, sorry. His name WAS Jazz. I shall call him Monty and he shall be my forever friend," Scarlet answered, in her cute-baby-animal voice.

"If he gets off this leash again then you can have him as your forever friend," he responded with a grin.

Scarlet faked a sigh and put the puppy on the ground so he could run back to his owner.

"My name is Monty," the man said, leaning down to clip the leash onto Jazz's collar.

Scarlet turned all the way around to look at him.

"Just kidding…but now that I have your attention…"

"Ah…impressive," Scarlet said. "Ok. I'll bite. What do you have for me, Monty?"

"What about dinner with me…and Jazz…tonight?"

"So, using your dog to meet unsuspecting women in the park…that's your thing?"

"No," he laughed. "This is the first time. Is it working?"

Scarlet thought about it for a moment. She didn't have anything else to do. That was a pretty adorable 'meet-cute'…and if anything went wrong, she could always kill him.

"That sounds like a good idea," she answered.

She stood up to meet him, face-to-face and to size him up…just in case.

He was attractive, in his late forties with salt and pepper hair. He wore stylish glasses and his clothes and shoes were expensive.

"My name is Sterling," he said.

"You're kidding, right? 'Monty' is more believable."

He laughed.

"It is really Sterling. I'll let you see my driver's license."

"Ok, Sterling. My name is Veronica and you can't see my driver's license.

• • • • • •

They spent the evening on the patio of an eccentric restaurant by the bay that had a separate menu for dogs…and an impressive vegetarian menu for Scarlet.

Sterling was an architect, divorced and his wit matched Scarlet's. They had a lot in common and it felt very natural that they ended up back at his penthouse for drinks.

They talked long into the evening and eventually ended up in bed.

He didn't drive Scarlet wild, but it was something she could work with. If she'd had more time, she certainly could have taught him how to develop his natural talents.

…but she didn't have the time.

He awoke to a note from Veronica, thanking him for a wonderful evening.

It was an evening that he never forgot.

He was disappointed that she didn't leave any contact information and he and Jazz looked for her at the park every time they went.

…but they never saw her again.

In another world, where "meet-cutes" are real and Scarlet wasn't a vigilante, she would have enjoyed getting to know Sterling and Jazz.

In her time with them, she saw what she could have had…had her life been normal.

…had she not been born into hell; a damaged doll being jerked around by a demented Puppet King.

Chapter 3: Sweet Home

Leo hated Alabama. Though he grew up in the south - and loved it - Alabama represented all the worst parts the south had to offer...and he avoided it at all cost.

...but this is where she was from. He was sure of it.

The highways looked different and there were businesses where the woods had been, but he was still able to track down the general area where he had first picked Scarlet up.

From there, he worked backward.

She would've had to have been walking along the river for hours before she made it to the highway because during that time, the closest town was miles away.

Would everything have turned out differently if he hadn't given her a ride that night...or if he hadn't left her in New Orleans to be raised by the streets?

God works in mysterious ways, no doubt. How else could this unbelievable story have come to be?

...but had he played his role correctly?

Was he really supposed to save this girl from who-knows-what in the woods in Alabama and then send her on her way to kill men up and down the coasts...and everywhere in between...and then have to be the one to track her down and bring her to justice?

Sometimes, I think you're a twisted son-of-a-bitch, he thought looking up into the heavens.

After a few missteps and false alarms, he finally found the area he believed she was from.

It was deadland. The houses were barely standing, and it looked like it had always been that way. Old paint was faded and even the grass looked lifeless. Windows were broken and buildings abandoned.

He could see where there once had been a general store and there was still a church, of course but the streets were dead.

Leo pulled up to the first old house he saw that showed signs of life.

The house itself was crumbling but two plump women sat on the porch, rocking and fanning themselves. Neither heard of anyone named Scarlet from back in those days but they did have an interesting tale about an old man and a young girl that had lived on Briarberry Lane.

The next house reported the same.

…and the next.

They pointed him in the direction of the house where the old man and the girl had lived.

The house on Briarberry had been condemned long ago but was still standing. The grass was overgrown and there was a large field beside it that hadn't been maned in years.

Two concrete steps with wild honeysuckle growing on either side lead up to the porch. Leo barely had to push the front door to get inside. It was dark and it smelled foul. It was considered haunted by the people in the town but even in its best day, this had been a place of nightmares.

The house was at least a hundred years old. It was falling apart at the seams and the floor sagged beneath his feet when he walked.

He opened the door that led to what must have been her bedroom. It was the size of a large closet and there was a dirty mattress on the floor. Animals had eaten through pieces of it and it was dry rotted.

There was a lock on the outside of the bedroom door and the windows had been painted black from the outside. Leo felt physically sick as he realized: this hadn't just been hell for her, it had been a prison.

He retreated to the kitchen and looked around.

This is where she was when she had finally had enough…where she was when she took her life into her own hands.

He had learned from the townspeople that she had beaten him with his own belt…a belt she had likely been beaten with many times. Leo looked around and he could see it in his mind.

…he could see everything that happened there.

He rushed out the door with tears in his eyes and threw up all over the honeysuckle.

By the time Leo drove out of Alabama, he had the answers he came for…but not what he expected.

There had been a girl in the town…beautiful beyond words with dark hair and crystal eyes, just as Leo thought there would be.

…and she disappeared around the same time that he met Scarlet.

Most everyone he spoke to hoped she had gotten away…and many reveled in the victory that she might have been the one who killed the old man, after all.

…but her name wasn't Scarlet.

Her name was never Scarlet.

......

She placed the cupcake on a plate and pushed the candle down into the fluffy pink icing. She licked icing off her finger then struck the lighter and lit the wick.

Scarlet didn't know exactly when her birthday was. Her father never celebrated a birthday for her. She didn't have any grandparents. She never went to school. She was nothing more than a prisoner but every year, her father would mention that she was another year older.

No cupcake.

No wish.

It wasn't even on the same day every year.

…but she knew it was sometime in June, so every year on June 5^{th,} Scarlet celebrated, by herself, with a cupcake and a bottle from the top shelf.

"Happy Birthday, baby," she said to herself.

Then she pursed her lips together and blew out the flame.

......

Scarlet was getting tired of moving around again. It had been almost a year since Leo tracked her down in Colorado. She missed William and Levi - her family. She missed her home.

The only thing that made her happy about leaving them, was knowing that after the divorce was finalized, William and Levi would be together. It was their time to live out loud.

She didn't realize how much working in the clubs had kept her from getting bored all those years, when traveling from city to city was her way of life. Sight-seeing and sitting around in hotels were sucking the life out of her. She was too old for the clubs, too old for drugs and too young to die.

Maybe I should turn myself in now, she thought. *Go find Leo and just hand myself over to him. Or maybe take myself completely out of the game. Go see the Puppet King and tell him to suck my dick.*

The feelings of loneliness brought the memories of all the people she lost. She would replay them again and again in her mind.

When she went out to see the city, grab a drink or hunt down a meatless meal, she would watch the families: the mother tucking her daughter's hair behind her ear and the little boy holding his father's hand to cross the street.

In her life, Scarlet had never been that child nor would she ever be that parent.

Sometimes, she found sex and sometimes she found murder…but Scarlet could never find home.

......

"This is a lovely place you have," Scarlet said, motioning to the extravagant décor.

"Thanks. I can't take credit. My wife hired a decorator. Cost me a fortune," he answered.

He poured two glasses of whiskey over ice and handed one to Scarlet.

Her wig was short and blonde – very Marilyn, as was her red halter dress. She sat on the black velour couch, folding her legs underneath her with her ankles crossed, but taking care not to let her heels touch the furniture.

"So, where is your wife?" Scarlet asked as if she didn't already know.

Scarlet was very thorough when stalking her victims. She didn't overlook anything, and she never made mistakes. So, when she asked questions, she always knew the answer.

Allowing them the opportunity to tell the truth was all part of the game…but their answer didn't really matter.

If Scarlet was there, then they were guilty…and their fate had been decided before they ever met her.

"She's uh…"

…*buried under the roses in the back yard*, Scarlet thought.

"…she is spending some time out of the country. I was uh…" he stammered, drinking deeply from his glass. "I wasn't faithful. I upset her."

Scarlet emptied her glass as well and stood up, motioning to the bar area of the living room. She took his glass and crossed the room to fill them up again.

Behind them the water of the pool sparkled through the glass of the living room windows. Large green-leafed plants and delicate purple flowers lined the yard. In the back center, looming and staring at them, was the rose-covered grave of a woman who didn't deserve to die.

Scarlet made sure he was watching her body when she walked back with his drink. She pressed it into his hand and sat in his lap.

"Drink up, baby," she said in a sultry voice.

He gulped his drink down his throat as quickly as he had the first.

"She never wanted to have sex...so I mean, obviously I had to get it somewhere else," he said, pulling at his tie.

Scarlet started unbuttoning his shirt.

"Is it hot in here...to you, Lori? Should I..." he trailed off and shook his head.

Scarlet stood and put her hand on his face.

"It's ok, baby. That's just the drug kicking in," she whispered. "I spiked your drink."

......

He awoke to his own drowning.

His body was above water, on the pavement, but his head was being held down. He tried to fight against it, but he couldn't. Just when he was ready to give up, his head was pulled from the water.

"Why did you do it?" a calm voice asked.

"Lori?" he asked, confused.

"My name isn't Lori, you idiot. It's Scarlet. I've been sent from hell to collect your soul," she answered, laughing.

She pulled his head up so he was looking directly at the roses. Fear rushed over him.

"That woman sacrificed everything for you. She gave up her career, moved far away from her family...all so you could take her life and bury her the way other people bury their pets...in the fucking backyard?"

"I...I'm..." he started.

"Shut the fuck up, Dick. You don't mind if I call you Dick...do you Richard?

"I...I'm..."

"Just kidding. I'm going to call you whatever I want to call you," she said laughing.

She pushed his head back underwater. He tried to scream but it only made him feel like he was drowning faster.

She yanked his head up again.

Water ran down his face in a sheet and he coughed more of it out of his lungs. He started crying and choking.

"I never ask questions I don't already know the answers to," Scarlet continued. "You killed her for the insurance money. She found out about your affairs and she wanted a divorce. All she did for you...and you couldn't just let her have her share and walk away to find a better man. You had to end her life…and now I'm going to end yours…on her behalf."

Scarlet pulled his head up so he could see the rose bushes one last time and then she held his head under water, riding his writhing body like a pony, laughing the entire.

••••••

Chapter 4: Inside and Out

Scarlet was spending far too much time inside her own mind.

It was a dark place becoming darker by the day.

There had never been any chance that her life would have a happy ending. Her story had been written as a tragedy from the beginning.

Pain.

Sorrow.

Madness.

Scarlet had accepted what was obvious to her: from birth she was meant to be tortured and to torture. She was created by The Puppeteer with this life in mind and there was no escape from her destiny.

...but who would she have been had she not been destined to be who she was? In an alternate universe, had she grown up with a loving mother instead of being beaten down and used by her father?

Would she have a normal life in a normal town...inside a house that wasn't built on nightmares?

Would she have a husband like Sterling, and would they take their dog on walks in the park and eat at dog-friendly restaurants by the bay on Saturday nights?

Ultimately, it didn't matter what could have been. It only mattered what was real in Scarlet's world.

…and Scarlet was, once again, where she always ended up: alone with only her memories and her thoughts.

Dark thoughts looming in a dark mind can only lead to more of the same.

……

Leo's mind was always on Scarlet.

Even in his dreams he was hunting her.

Since his trip to Alabama, he had become more obsessed with the girl who grew up in the house of horrors on Briarberry.

He remembered the bruises and scrapes he could see when he picked her up on that night in 1974. The rest of her body was covered…so God only knows what other injuries were underneath.

…and the emotional injuries…those never went away.

He wished he had gone to her childhood home years ago because he finally understood her, at least.

He looked at the map on his wall…his Scarlet Map. The dots represented murders, yes, but she hadn't just been killing strip club patrons and associates. She had been ending the lives of rapists, murderers and pedophiles.

She had been killing men like her father.

Was she doing it for her own pleasure? Was she punishing the guilty…or was she, in her mind, saving others from the fate she had already met as a child?

Maybe it was for all those reasons.

In another world, Leo thought he would just let her go…but here, in his reality, he couldn't let her go.

He had to find her.

● ● ● ● ● ●

She was in a bar when she overheard two women behind her discussing rape.

It isn't an uncommon discussion for women to have. One in five women has an experience that can be classified as rape. Even when they choose not to report it, they sometimes share with friends.

Scarlet listened for the name and for the details.

…and then she found him.

He was a security guard. He used his uniform to throw women off guard and then raped them in the parking lot.

Scarlet stalked him for a week.

She orchestrated an 'accidental' meeting.

Then she lured him, as he had lured so many women, into the darkest part of the parking garage where there were no cameras.

She stabbed him in the heart and cut his dick off.

He tried to scream but Scarlet put her hand over his mouth.

"It's ok, baby," she whispered. "Just relax and go with it. You know this is what you wanted. You know you were asking for it."

• • • • • •

They met at the hotel bar and the attraction was immediate.

"Come to my room with me?" the practical stranger had asked over their fourth round of drinks.

Scarlet didn't have to think twice.

She was very enticing. She was wearing a navy plaid skirt and a lowcut cashmere sweater that was the same color blue as her eyes. Her hair was red, and her nails were long.

They were barely in the door before Scarlet pulled her into her body and kissed her with fervor, winding her fingers through her long, red hair. She grabbed her ass with both hands and pulled her in even closer.

"I still haven't told you my name…" the woman started, her blue eyes searching Scarlet's.

"Shhhh," Scarlet whispered, running her thumb along her bottom lip and then kissing her again.

"No names. Just this," she breathed, slowly pulling up the redhead's skirt.

"You're fucking gorgeous," she said, opening the buttons on Scarlet's blouse.

They undressed each other, went to bed, and pleasured one other for hours. Neither slept until the first morning light peaked through the edge of the closed curtains.

When the redhead awoke that afternoon, she was alone but didn't have a single regret. No one had ever taken her on a ride like that. The beautiful dark-haired beauty with the crystal eyes had fulfilled her beyond her wildest dreams.

It was the most exciting night of her life.

· · · · · · · ·

Leo laid beside the blonde he had just fucked, unfulfilled, wondering if it was ok to leave. He imagined she hadn't had a good time either. His mind had been elsewhere all evening.

His mind was always elsewhere…but it had been so much worse since he got back from Alabama.

Her name isn't even fucking Scarlet, he thought. *She's basically a fucking ghost. No records of her anywhere…*

"Penny for your thoughts?" the top-heavy blonde asked, sitting up beside him.

"Sorry, darlin'. I guess my mind is on work," he replied pushing her hair back from her eyes.

"Maybe I can help," she said playfully and reached under the blankets to stroke him awake again.

He wanted to protest because his mind was still on Scarlet but that's exactly why he couldn't. When he closed his eyes, instead of the blonde, it was Scarlet - just as she had looked in Atlanta six years ago.

It was Scarlet handling his cock and readying it for her mouth. She looked up at him with her dark hair covering part of her perfect porcelain face, her green eyes with the yellow ring around the pupil locking with his…

"Fuck!" Leo yelled, sitting up straight and almost pushing the woman – the real woman he was in bed with - away.

What the fuck was that, he thought frantically. *What. The. Fuck.*

He was rock hard.

"Ok!" the blonde squealed, unaware of Leo's intrusive thoughts.

Leo tried to clear his head of Scarlet's face – of her body – as the blonde lowered herself onto him.

…but even with his eyes open, she was still there.

"Fuck me, baby," Scarlet said in Leo's ear. "Fuck me the way you've always wanted to."

Unable to tame his mind, Leo grabbed Scarlet by her waist, lifting his hips up hard toward her body. He fucked Scarlet all night, giving her everything he had until he exploded inside her.

It was the most exciting night of his life.

......

Leo had been obsessed and now he was addicted.

He found new women and turned them into Scarlet in his mind, enjoying every inch of her beautiful body with his eyes, his hands and his mouth.

Loving her from the inside…

He no longer cared that it didn't make sense…or that it might not be right. He wanted her. He needed her.

…and this was the only way.

It had been weeks of living out these fantasies, so he questioned his sanity when he saw her sitting right in front of him at a dive bar in Atlanta.

He blinked and then blinked again.

It was Scarlet.

It was **his** fucking Scarlet.

Her hair, hanging down her bare back was a little shorter and a little lighter than it had been since he had last seen her, pissed off and yelling at him in her apartment in Atlanta.

He was nervous and excited as he approached.

Is this really happening? He thought.

"Is this seat taken, darlin'?" he asked, standing close enough to take in her scent.

She smelled like roses…just like he remembered.

"It's yours," Scarlet answered. "That voice sounds like home."

She turned on her barstool, flashed that million-dollar smile and said, "hello, Leo. I've been waiting for you, baby."

Chapter 5: Irrevocably Yours

"So...why now? Why are you ready to talk to me now? You obviously could have found me anytime you wanted to. Why didn't you come to me before? I could have helped you."

"I did go to you. You are the only person I ever went to for help, Leo. Sinepet..."

"I'm sorry I let you down, Scar-" Leo stopped short.

"Yeah...I know you went to Alabama, baby...to visit the shithole I escaped. So, you know that's not my name...and you know I killed my father."

Scarlet lifted her glass in the air, then drew it to her lips and threw the contents back.

"Yes, but I also know what happened to you there. I know **why** you killed your father; I know why you killed all of them."

"Does that change things for you?" she asked the question playfully, but she wanted the truth.

Leo didn't answer right away. He wanted to know everything before he gave up anything.

"Why now? Why are you talking to me now?" Leo asked.

"Why haven't you arrested me?" she shot back.

He was quiet.

"Because you lost your badge?" she challenged.

"No. I mean…yes. I can't arrest you without a badge but that's not why."

She looked past his eyes and into his soul for answers.

"I'm sorry I fucked up your marriage, Leo…but I didn't want you to catch me so I'm kind of glad I fucked up your job," she winked.

She looked so sexy when she spoke…when she winked. His belly flipped…and she saw it in his eyes.

"Leo!" she squealed, laughing. "You want to fuck me!"

"What? No…Scar - " Leo shifted uncomfortably in his seat.

"Baaaby," she drew out the word slowly, seductively, "I know that look," her eyes drove into him now, "and you can still call me Scarlet. Perhaps she never was…but she is who I am…and who I have been. The girl I was…the name my father called me…she died with him."

Leo didn't know what to say.

"It's ok. I never met a straight man that didn't want to fuck me," Scarlet refused to break eye contact.

This was a game to her now.

"I don't just want to fuck you, Scarlet. I mean…I absolutely want to fuck you…but there's more… I'm in love with you," Leo said, intensifying their eye contact and leaning toward her, "I think I have been since I saw you in that strip club in Atlanta."

Scarlet stopped smiling and swallowed hard.

Plot twist, she thought. *Still at it, you sick puppet bastard?*

She had never thought of Leo that way before…and she wasn't sure that she could now. She had been running from him since Atlanta…he had been chasing her since Atlanta.

She was a killer…and he was the cops.

No.

"That's ridiculous. You don't even fucking know me," Scarlet replied as coolly as she could.

…but he did. He knew her since the beginning.

"Darlin', I know you better than any person – living or dead - ever has or ever will. I'm the only person who knows you well enough to know where the bodies are buried."

Scarlet laughed.

"Shows what you know. I didn't bury any," she said as she motioned to the bartender for another round.

Leo smiled. It was true, she hadn't buried any of them. She always left them right where they were, for the world to see.

God, she's fucking gorgeous, he thought looking her over.

He couldn't believe she was there, right in front of him.

I never want to move from this spot. I want to stay here forever with this fucking brutal-ass vigilante who could end my life if she wanted to.

She was wearing a red shirt that dipped low in the front with thin straps on her shoulders. He knew he would barely have to pull the straps down and the whole shirt would drop... her jeans were tight...he couldn't wait to peel them off her...

She snapped her fingers in his face.

"Stop, undressing me with your eyes, you dirty old man."

He looked a little embarrassed but also amused.

"Old man, huh?"

"So, what's your plan then, Leo? Run off into the sunset...the misunderstood serial killer and the sexy FBI agent live happily ever after?" she asked mockingly and pushed his shot glass toward him.

"That isn't fair," Leo said, throwing his shot back and motioning to the bartender for another round.

"Fair? Nothing is fucking fair," Scarlet snipped.

"Well, maybe not," Leo said, pushing her hair back from her face, "but you just accidentally called me sexy, so I think I might actually have a shot here," he smiled.

"This isn't funny, Leo."

"I know it isn't. It's terrifying. I'm just coming to terms with it. I don't expect you to decide anything right now," he said pulling her onto her feet and in between his legs where he still sat on the barstool.

"Will you spend the night with me tonight?"

"Leo...I..."

"Do you have other plans?" he asked.

"Well...I was going to kill this guy...but..."

Leo looked at her sternly.

He really was a sexy man.

"You think shit is funny...then I have jokes too. Ok...no, I don't have plans. I came to see you because I knew you'd be here. I've been stalking you for weeks."

"Weeks?" Leo thought of where all he had been – who all he had been with – over the last few weeks...all in search of her...and she had been there all along.

"Spend the night with me, Scarlet. Your rules. You choose what happens and you can leave whenever you want."

Scarlet laughed.

"Oh, baby, I know I can leave whenever I want. No man can stop me. Not even you."

......

Scarlet got a bottle to go from the bartender and she and Leo walked outside to his car.

"You are used to getting almost everything you want, huh?"

Scarlet opened the bottle, took a huge sip and handed it to Leo.

"Yeah. I think it's the Puppet King's way of making up for the first 15 years of my life."

"The puppet...?"

"You probably call him God. Most people do...but my puppeteer, he doesn't have an arch nemesis like a comic book character. There is no biblical devil. There is only the Puppet King, pulling all the strings...and he is a sick son-of-a-bitch."

She motioned to the two of them as proof.

"Ah...I get why he would feel like a puppeteer to you."

"Really?" Scarlet asked, genuinely shocked.

"I mean, yeah, you had a rough go of it until you took matters into your own hands…and even then, you've had some of the hardest of times. I can see how it would feel like someone else is pulling the strings."

"Leonard McAvoy," she said in her fake southern accent as she pushed herself up onto the hood of his car. "If I didn't know any better, I'd think you were trying to get lucky tonight."

Leo stayed a safe distance until Scarlet motioned him to her.

"Oh, I'm already feeling pretty lucky, Ms. Scarlet," Leo came back with an exaggerated southern accent of his own. "I'm just happy to be here, right now, with you, after all these years."

Scarlet grabbed his shirt and pulled him in. She wrapped her arms around his neck and her legs around his waist.

"Since you're being so kind," she continued in her drawl, "I think you should take me back to your room and have your way with me."

"Yes, ma'am," Leo responded.

She pressed her lips against his. Slowly, at first….pulling back to look at his face. Then, their mouths met fully, their tongues reaching for each other and a thousand fireworks exploded inside their heads.

⋯⋯

The door of Leo's hotel room flung open and Leo stumbled inside with Scarlet's legs wrapped around his hips. He awkwardly closed the door behind him and turned to hold Scarlet against it.

He pulled the thin red straps down over her shoulders – just as he had wanted to at the bar. He made a guttural sound in his throat at the sight of her.

She was perfection…better than any fantasy.

Seeing how excited he was made Scarlet excited too.

Leo put her down and dropped to his knees to unbutton her pants. He started to pull them down…he could see the lace at the top of her panties…but she stopped him.

"Slow down, tiger," she purred. "I didn't know I wanted this…but now I do…so let's make it last."

Leo smiled up at her.

"You don't have much faith in me," he said, peeling down her jeans and hooking his finger in the top of her panties.

"Oh, I do, love..." she said. That's why I want to enjoy every second…of every minute…of every hour…"

"…of every day," he continued as he pulled her panties down.

"…of every week…" he said and licked her once.

"of every month…" he continued and licked her again.

"Leo…we won't…"

Leo took her into his mouth, and she gasped…pushing against him. Most men had to work hard to please Scarlet with their tongues and few could bring her to completion.

"Leo…I…"

Leo grabbed her hips, spun her body around so she was facing the door, bent her over and didn't stop using his mouth until she called The Puppeteer by his common name.

......

The first few days seemed like one long day to both of them. They only went out for food if they had to.

Leo devoured every inch of Scarlet's body and she devoured every inch of his.

They laughed.

They shared stories.

It all felt so…normal.

…and that was worrisome for Scarlet. She knew normal never lasted for long.

"Where do you go when you stare into space?" Leo asked her.

"I'm thinking about reality…our reality…outside this time and place."

"This is reality."

"No, baby. This is still fantasy. This is still make-believe. Reality happens when we walk out that door and into the world."

"You had a normal life with William and Levi. We could have that, Scarlet."

Scarlet laughed.

"I killed someone every time we went on vacation, Leo. I strangled a man in Miami. Pushed another off a balcony in New York. They didn't know, of course. They are good men – William and Levi. You are a good man, baby. I am...I will always be...this."

"You don't have to be whatever it is you think you are anymore. You can stop. You can leave it behind you..."

She smiled and kissed him.

"...but you would always know...and if it catches up with me..."

"It won't. We will figure it out."

"You are an FBI agent, Leo..."

"So...I won't be any more, then."

"Silly man. People can't just stop being who they are."

"Come home with me, Scarlet," he said with desperation in his voice.

"To your sad apartment with your Scarlet map on the wall?" she laughed.

"How do you know about the Scarlet map? and no… the Scarlet map is here. I never leave town without it."

"Shut the fuck up! Let me see it!" she exclaimed excitedly. "I had one, but I burned it."

Leo got up to get the map from his bag and Scarlet slapped him on the ass.

"I've kept up with you too, Leo. I saw the map when I tracked you to your apartment after you found me in Colorado. To think, all this time, I was running from you …and all I had to do was confront you and fuck you to get you to stop chasing me."

"Easy now," he said. "I think there was a time I would have taken you into custody…but maybe not. It all feels so confusing now."

He spread the map out across the bed.

"Wow," Scarlet's eyes widened. "Has anyone ever seen this?"

"No. I tried, in the beginning to tell people about you. Everyone thought I was crazy. They still do."

"Normally, I'm offended when men consistently underestimate women, but in this instance, it has worked tremendously in my favor."

She patted the bed for him to sit beside her.

"You're missing a few."

She pointed to New Orleans.

"The first person I killed after my father was here. It was many years after. He killed the love of my life and destroyed my dreams."

"Vasco. I'm so sorry. Were there more...in New Orleans?"

"No...I never went back."

"What if I had never left you there?"

"I was a child. You were a man. Our entire relationship would have been different...and never, ever changed into this...and I like this. I'm glad we have this. Right here. Right now."

She grabbed his dick and teased the side of his mouth with her tongue.

"I should have protected you."

"You couldn't have."

"Well, I can now."

"You still can't...but there are a lot of things you can do **to** me, baby," she continued as she crawled into his lap.

She draped her legs across either side of his body and used both hands to guide him inside her.

He closed his eyes, sighed and pressed his forehead to hers.

"Stop being sad about things that already happened…or things that haven't happened yet, baby," she said. "Be here with me now."

"Scarlet…"

"Leo…fuck me, right now, like you mean it…and I'll go home with you."

Leo's whole face lit up.

…and he meant it.

He meant it several times.

Chapter 6: Until We Meet Again

Leo's apartment was typical of a bachelor's home.

He had only the barest of essentials and no art anywhere. Scarlet only made it two days before she suggested they go shopping.

"Men don't need the same things women do to be happy," Leo insisted.

Scarlet made him touch different towels so he could feel the difference and choose between what appeared to him to be two of the same shades of blue.

"You aren't happy," she said laughing. "No one is happy with bare walls. You need beautiful things to look at...luxurious things to touch. Your home should be comfortable. You should **want** to be there."

"Well, I'm happier now and I really want to go home with you," he said trying to pull her in...but she slapped his hand away playfully.

She piled towels and sheets in his arms and found a lush comforter.

"What else do you have to do with your money?"

That was a fair question. Leo did have a decent amount of money saved and had inherited even more when his father passed away.

"Ok, darlin'. Whatever you want. Let's do it."

. . . . . .

Leo had Scarlet bent over the bed when the phone rang.

He reluctantly let her go with one of his hands and reached for the phone...never taking his eyes off her ass.

She continued to push back against him until she heard the gruff voice of his boss on the line. She pulled away and slid out from underneath him. He tried to pull her back, but she rolled over, and he saw the look on her face.

He hurriedly finished his conversation, hung up the phone, and tried to pull her back in again.

"Baby, please," he started, "I see where your mind is going. Don't."

"Leo..."

"Scarlet, stop."

He tried to kiss her, but she pulled away...so he let her go. Scarlet wasn't the kind of woman that took kindly to being manhandled...and Leo wasn't the kind of man to handle a woman if she didn't specifically say she wanted it.

They had been enjoying playing house in his apartment, hidden away from the rest of the world. Inside his home, it almost seemed like they could be normal....like they were normal.

...but there was nothing normal about this situation.

She was a serial killer and he was an FBI agent, specializing in cold cases…primarily hers. There was no way it could end well. Maybe in another world or in another lifetime things could have been different…in a different story, where everyone has a happily ever after.

…but this was The Puppeteer's show and Scarlet was his favorite marionette.

……

"You're in danger as long as I'm here, Leo."

"You bet your fine ass I am. You are the most dangerous woman in the fucking world."

Scarlet rolled her eyes.

Leo paused…his woman was in no mood for jokes.

"I was the only person looking for you…and now I've got you, Scarlet. You are mine. There is no one else coming for you. There is no one coming for me. We are safe here," Leo soothed, zipping up his suit bag.

Leo's boss had asked to see him, so Leo had to go.

"I will only be gone for a few days for work and then I'm coming back for you…not with a SWAT team…just me. Just you and me. Always. Do you trust me?"

"It doesn't matter if I trust you. You can't trust me. I can't stop. If I stop then these men will continue to get away. If I don't stop then you will eventually get tangled up and you'll lose everything."

He pulled Scarlet into his lap.

"We can't save all the women…and you can't kill all the men, darlin'. It is a hard acceptance…knowing that people are hurting, and you can't stop it, but law enforcement has to accept it as part of the job every day."

"Yes, you do…but I don't."

......

As it were with every man she had ever encountered, Scarlet's target in the Armani suit was an easy catch. She barely had to cast her net and it took almost no effort to lure him from the bar and into the newly vacant building down the street.

She only had to allude to a risqué rendezvous to get him into the office she had prepared for them. Once inside, she removed his jacket, unbuttoned his shirt and he drunkenly complied while she tied him to a chair.

She lifted her dress and straddled him, making sure he could feel her warmth through his slacks. She gently touched the back of his neck and pushed another pill from her tongue to his.

His excitement was building, his dick growing in his pants, so it took him a moment to catch on when she whispered in his ear "I have so many things to tell you before you die."

The look of confusion – and then panic – was one Scarlet knew well. It excited her in ways she couldn't emulate in any other arena of life.

He struggled against the binds that held him securely to the desk chair, but he couldn't move...and the drugs were weighing him down.

"Sit tight, little mouse. There's no escape. The pussy cat has you in her clutches and she wants to play," Scarlet laughed and grinded against him.

"Wait...what happened?" Scarlet asked, pretending to be surprised.

She faked a frown, reached between his legs and stroked his cock. She squeezed it, hard, and he winced.

"Where did it go? Ugh...you men are all the same. Only excited when you think you'll get to pound the pussy. No one likes it when they find out that the pussy is doing the pounding."

Scarlet smiled, punched him in the face, grabbed his hair, pulled his head back and said "Look at me..."

....

"This guy...he's a real piece of fucking work," Leo's boss said beneath his bushy mustache.

He put down the newspaper and Leo saw the story he had been reading was the same one everyone had been talking about. Fred Holloway, a con man who made millions from stealing from unsuspecting investors had been accused of 26 counts of sexual abuse...and had been found not guilty on all counts.

"Indeed, boss. Is that why you wanted to see me?"

"No," he answered, sliding Leo's badge across the desk. "You are reinstated. You can pick up your gun downstairs…but no more crazy talk…and stay away from The Strip Club Killer case. It's on hold indefinitely."

"You got it! Thank you, sir. Sorry I got a little too…obsessed."

"It happens to the best of us, Leo. Just remember tunnel-vision will betray even the best agent."

Leo, overjoyed, headed for the door. He couldn't wait to get home to tell Scarlet that they could have a life together.

Finally, after all these years, they could be happy.

Together.

Leo's boss picked up the newspaper again and said, "you know, he was an associate of Sinepet. Too bad that stripper of yours never had this piece of shit Holloway in her sights."

His hand froze on the doorknob and his heart dropped in his chest.

Fuck.

. . . .

Leo rushed through the door of his apartment, but just as he knew she would be, Scarlet was gone.

He had gotten his badge back.

They had given him back his gun.

...but all he wanted was her.

He slammed his fist down on the counter and looked around. He knew she had been here because his apartment had been completely redecorated with her help, but every physical trace of Scarlet had been wiped away as if she had never been to his apartment.

...as if she had never existed.

Which, he was reminded, she never had. Scarlet wasn't a real person according to any database...and his chances of finding the woman he was in love with...the woman who had made herself into Scarlet... were next to none.

"She took the fucking map", he said aloud.

Leo bolted out the door and slid into the driver's seat. He knew, for the first time since he began his quest, where she would strike next...**who** she would strike next.

He had been waiting for this day for years...but everything was different now.

The way he wanted her was different.

What would he do when he found her now?

Pick her up like a caveman and drag her away?

Take her back home and lock her up in a room so she could never get away?

No…Scarlet had already been treated like property. She didn't deserve to be treated that way again. She didn't deserve to be locked away in a prison either.

Nothing made sense.

…not his obsession with her…not his addiction to her.

Why of all the women in the world…why was he in love with fucking Scarlet?

......

A few cops stood outside the building, as the flames died down.

"So, what's going on in there?" asked one of the late arrivals.

"Pretty brutal, man. That guy from the news…"

"Fred Holloway, the millionaire acquitted on all those rape charges?"

"Yep, that's him. Well…was him. He's dead as hell. Stabbed, set on fire…dick hanging out and everything. Terrible."

"Shit," the man said. "The perp…he got away?"

"Nah, man. It was a female. She's dead too. Body burned to a crisp…but we've got an ID. Her purse made it though. They also found a journal and a map…looks like she killed a bunch of other dudes."

. . . .

Leo had been listening to everything he could on the police radio in his car. There were two bodies and one was a female…a female who appeared to be the killer.

Please, no. Please don't be her.

He screeched into the parking lot.

He jumped the police tape and pushed past everyone, shoving his badge into their faces.

In his mind, he saw every moment with her, from the time he picked her up on a dark Alabama highway until he said goodbye to her, standing in the door of his apartment in Virginia.

There were so many things he should have done differently. So many choices that he wished he could be faced with again so he could make the right ones this time.

The walk from the door of the office to the body bags felt like it happened in slow motion. Leo's heart was pounding in his chest and his feet were made of lead.

He motioned and they unzipped the bag. It was a male. It was Holloway.

He moved to the second bag and motioned again.

Tears filled his eyes.

It wasn't Scarlet.

......

He composed himself and surveyed the scene as he would have any other crime scene. She had wrapped everything up for him in a nice little package.

He would finally receive recognition from his boss and be praised for all his insight. The killer would be put to rest...and with her, all the cases marked on the map.

"Scarlet, huh? Helluva name for a Lady Killer," Leo said as he handed the ID back to the captain.

He stood outside the building until long after everyone was gone.

He thought he could still smell her – the faint fragrance of roses – in the air.

There was a moment he thought he felt someone rush past him but when he turned there was only darkness.

She was gone.

·······

Before the fire, Scarlet was a woman unhinged.

She had been torturing Holloway for hours…punishing him for the torture she had lived through all her life…but there was no satisfaction this time.

"I'm so sick and fucking tired of this, Armani," she said as she stuffed a scarf into his mouth. "I'm sick of living this life. I'm sick of looking over my shoulder."

She crossed the room and pulled a blanket from the corner revealing the body of a woman underneath.

Holloway tried to cry out but choked on the scarf.

"Stop crying, asshole," she said over her shoulder.

Scarlet sighed as she removed the wig from her head and placed it on the dead body.

"I didn't kill her. I'm not a monster, you stupid fuck. I…coerced… a man who works at the morgue into giving her to me."

Scarlet stroked the dead woman's forehead.

"She was no one to the world…isn't that sad, Armani? No one reported her missing. No one claimed her. No one wanted to know what happened. She had no dental records to trace. It's like she never existed.

They found her on the street, dead...and that's all there was to her story...so I am giving her a better one.

Her story will be told in every newspaper in the country.

She will be famous and generations from now, they will still know her name.

She is Scarlet."

....

"So, there she was with her boobs out, me and my buddies standing around waiting…" he started but was interrupted by the message over the intercom speaker:

"Mesdames et messieurs, votre vol pour Paris, France atterrira sous peu…"

"I wish they'd speak English. I mean we just left America so most of us on this plane are Americans," he stated arrogantly.

She pulled her glasses off and licked her full lips.

"She is just saying that we will land soon. Tell me, s'il vous plaît, what was your name, again?" she asked in a French accent.

"It's Chuck," he answered confidently.

"Of course, it is," she giggled.

As he rattled on, she looked out the window of the plane at her new hunting ground. She thought of Vasco, Val, Ryin and Leo…her dear Leo…she would miss them all for the rest of her life.

…but then, with the grace she was known to have, she pushed them to the back of her mind and returned her attention to her new little mouse, Chuck.

Poor fucked Chuck, she thought, *I wish I could kill him now so he would just shut the fuck up…*

From the author…

Thank you for reading Scarlet's story. This work of fiction touches on real problems being faced in our society.

If you are suffering from domestic violence, human trafficking, substance abuse or mental illness, please don't suffer in silence. There are many of us who made it through…and you can too.

<u>**Toll Free Hotlines for 24/7 Assistance**</u>:

National Domestic Violence
1-800-799-7233

National Human Trafficking
1-888-373-7888

Substance Abuse and Mental Health Services (SAMHSA)
1-800-662-HELP (4357)